Second Term at

TREBIZON

Second Term at TREBIZON

ANNE DIGBY

EGMONT

EGMONT

We bring stories to life

Second Term at Trebizon
First published in Great Britain 1979
by W. H. Allen
This edition published 2016 by Egmont UK Limited
The Yellow Building, 1 Nicholas Road, London W11 4AN

ISBN 978 1 4052 8064 8

www.egmont.co.uk

A CIP catalogue record for this title is available from the British Library

62824/1

Typeset in Goudy Old Style by Avon DataSet Ltd, Bidford on Avon,
Warwickshire
Printed and bound in Great Britain by CPI Group

Stay safe online. Any website addresses listed in this book are correct
at the time of going to print. However, Egmont is not responsible
for content hosted by third parties.

Please be aware that online content can be subject to change and websites can
contain content that is unsuitable for children. We advise that all children are
supervised when using the internet.

CONTENTS

1 Before the Term Began   1

2 Three Secret Wishes   13

3 The Team is Picked   27

4 Rebecca Counts Her Blessings   41

5 The First Quarrel   51

6 Towards a Break-Up   64

7 The Election is On   77

8 A Dirty Election   89

9 Right Out On a Limb   104

10 A Visit to the Hilary   114

11 The Big Showdown   127

12 Headline News   142

13 The Result of the Music Scholarship   158

14 How the Wishes Turned Out   165

For Daisy

<u>ONE</u>
Before the Term Began

Rebecca Mason's second term at Trebizon School was to be full of surprises. It was going to be the term in which Tish Anderson behaved in a way that had everybody baffled, including Rebecca, and drove Sue Murdoch almost to despair.

Rebecca sensed there was something different about Tish, even before the new term began.

The Christmas holidays were nearly over and Rebecca was at a loose end. Her London friends had already gone back to their school and her father had flown back to his job in Saudi Arabia. Her mother was dashing around getting their little terraced house in south London ready for the new tenants, before seeing Rebecca off to school and then joining up with Mr Mason abroad.

The previous September, Rebecca had dreaded going away to Trebizon, a boarding school in the west country. At the time, she didn't know a soul there and she was going to be the only new girl in the Second Year. Now, waiting for her second term to begin, she felt differently about Trebizon. In Ishbel Anderson (who was known as Tish) and Sue Murdoch she had found the perfect friends. Tish and Sue had come to Trebizon as First Years and had been best friends from the start. But after a clash with a mighty Sixth Former called Elizabeth Exton, and a lot of drama and excitement, the other two had taken to Rebecca wholeheartedly and now they were a threesome.

It was Friday and Rebecca took it for granted that she wouldn't be meeting up with Tish and Sue again until the following Tuesday, on the London to Trebizon train. Sue lived right up in north London somewhere and Tish lived outside the city altogether.

So she was overjoyed when Sue rang her at home.

'Can you come for the weekend?' she asked. 'Tish is here already. I'm playing at a fairly crummy concert tomorrow afternoon, with Nicola Hodges – remember her? – but the main thing is that my parents are giving a party afterwards, you should see the food! Will your parents let you come? You can stay the night.'

'I'll go and ask!' said Rebecca.

Mrs Mason gave her permission at once and Rebecca returned to the phone. She felt pleased and excited.

'It's fine! I'll come to the concert, shall I? Where is it?'

'It's in a hall near Hendon Central underground station.'

'Hendon Central – that's straight through from here on the Northern Line!' said Rebecca.

'Tish can meet you outside the station at half-past two and bring you to the hall. The concert starts at three o'clock. Nicola and I will be trying to get our fiddles in tune. Don't expect anything good.'

'You can play as many wrong notes as you like,' said Rebecca. 'I won't be able to tell the difference.'

'That's exactly what Tish said!'

'Nicola Hodges – oh, I remember her now,' said Rebecca. 'She's in the First Year isn't she? I didn't know you knew her out of school.'

Nicola had flaxen hair in plaits and a round cherubic face. Like Sue, she was already good enough at the violin to be in the school orchestra, and she had played a solo at the school's Christmas concert.

'I *didn't* know her out of school,' said Sue. 'But last term I told her about this music place I go to in the holidays and the next thing I knew her father had got her into it. Then the two of us were chosen to play together at this concert tomorrow. There'll be lots of other turns, too, like recorders and ballet and tap.'

'Can't wait,' said Rebecca. 'Is Tish by the phone?'

'She's gone out,' said Sue. 'But don't worry. She's dying for you to come. She'll meet you all right.'

'Where's she gone?'

'Up to Hampstead. That Outer Space Art Exhibition.'

'*What?*' said Rebecca. 'The one that's been in the papers? Twisted lumps of metal suspended from the ceiling and flashing lights –'

'That's the one.'

'That's not like Tish!'

'She just marched out,' said Sue. Rebecca could tell that she, too, was baffled. 'Didn't seem to expect

4

anyone would want to come. Said she suddenly felt like going to it.'

'Hope Tish isn't changing for the worse,' said Rebecca solemnly.

That evening she ironed her best pale green angora wool sweater, which went well with her fair hair, and hummed to herself. Then she ironed her trousers.

'Shouldn't you wear something smarter for a party?' inquired Mrs Mason anxiously. 'They're very well off, aren't they?'

Howard Murdoch, Sue's father, was the chairman of a big company called Metternex, though Rebecca had only found that out by chance once.

'Dead casual – that's what Sue said. She should know.'

'I expect they live in a lovely house,' sighed Mrs Mason.

'I'll describe it to you in tiny detail when I get back, Mum,' promised Rebecca. 'Even what sort of washing machine they have.'

Mrs Mason laughed. It was true, she loved to know such things.

Next day, after an early lunch, Rebecca set off across the common.

The January skies were grey and the trees on the common were bare, but she was in high spirits. She wore a thick navy-blue duffel coat over her clothes, her fair hair cascading over the thrown-back hood. She carried her night things in her denim shoulder bag. The day was cold and she was pleased to get down into the warm underground station, and into the train.

When she emerged in north London, forty minutes later, Tish was waiting for her beyond the ticket barrier.

She looked the same old Tish all right, except that instead of school uniform she was wearing bright red ski pants and a heavy, patterned black-and-yellow long jumper with hood attached. Slung from her shoulder she carried a small cassette player in a bright blue case. The grin was as big as ever, the black curls still as bouncy, although her face had a slight winter pallor.

'What have we here?' exclaimed Rebecca,

6

pointing at the cassette recorder. 'You lucky thing!'

'Got it for Christmas,' said Tish. 'I thought we'd try and tape their duet for them! It's got a mike!'

The idea of recording Sue and Nicola's violin performance during the show appealed to Rebecca. As it turned out, it livened up the afternoon quite considerably.

Six budding ballerinas had come out on to the stage, and were dancing rather badly. According to the programme, Sue and Nicola would be on next. Tish sat fiddling with the cassette recorder in her lap, getting it ready. The tape was already half-filled with very tuneless pop music, Tish's favourite kind, which she had got from the radio earlier. She was trying to wind the tape on to a blank part, ready to record.

Unfortunately, she pressed the wrong button.

Suddenly, as the ballet reached its most delicate point, the hushed piano in the hall was drowned by loud, thumping pop music. People in the crowded hall turned at once, pulling threatening faces and making strangled shushing noises. Tish was so taken aback that the case slid right off her lap and under the chair in front, still thumping out the loud music. She rescued it and switched it off and the whole incident was over in a matter of seconds, but both girls were attacked by a giggling fit so severe that they had only just recovered their composure by the time Sue and Nicola appeared on the stage with their violins.

None of this was in the least untypical of Tish. Rebecca had no reason to think there was anything different about her at all.

The first slightly odd thing came during the interval.

Because the hall was so small and crowded, everybody had to stay in their seats, and cups of tea were brought round in paper cups. Rebecca and Tish talked about the holidays and then Rebecca, suddenly remembering, asked:

'What was the exhibition like?'

'What exhibition?' asked Tish.

'The funny one at Hampstead. Sue said you'd gone there yesterday. Was it weird and wonderful?'

Instead of laughing and joking about it, Tish just looked embarrassed. She stared down into her cup of tea.

'I didn't go to it after all. I just went for a walk.'

'Oh.'

There was an awkward silence. Rebecca tried to

pick up the threads of conversation again, but Tish seemed to be sunk in thought. It was almost as though Rebecca had, unwittingly, touched on a very tender spot. But why? How? Finally she gave up and just drank her tea in silence. What on earth had got into Tish?

Her eyes strayed down to the front of the hall. The front rows were reserved for the people in the concert, who could take a place there once their own performances were over. Sue was sitting there with Nicola. Earlier Sue had turned and waved and signalled to them, but now she and the flaxen-haired girl were deep in conversation, their heads bent close together.

Could Tish and Sue have quarrelled in the last couple of days? Rebecca wondered, groping for an explanation. Had Sue got thick with Nicola Hodges in the holidays, over this concert? Serious music wasn't exactly Tish's scene. Maybe she felt left out . . .

The lights dimmed and the second half of the concert began. A particularly bad rendering of 'Oh, for the wings of a dove,' by an elderly soprano began to revive Tish. Rebecca noticed her taping it, surreptitiously. By the end of the show she seemed her normal self again.

A lot of people piled into cars afterwards to go to the party at the Murdochs' home. The house was everything Rebecca's mother could have imagined, high on a hill and standing in its own grounds, with far-reaching views of the lights of London. Rebecca made mental notes of some of the lovely furnishings and fabrics, in order not to disappoint her mother.

The food, as Sue had promised, was everything that Rebecca could have imagined. The trifle was the most mouth-wateringly sweet concoction she had ever tasted, and the pastries had real cream in them.

Sue introduced Rebecca to her parents and her two brothers, David and Edward. Mrs Murdoch, like Sue herself, wore spectacles and had the same sandy-coloured hair, delicate features and high cheekbones. The boys were dark like their father. Howard Murdoch was a big man, who had played rugby for Cambridge in his youth. He had very thick beetling eyebrows that, like his head of hair, were black touched with grey. His face was craggy and strong-looking, yet kind. Rebecca could see why Sue adored him.

Nicola Hodges's parents were a surprise. They travelled with Nicola to the party in a rather battered old lorry which said *Hodges Road Haulage* on the side. Brian Hodges had had to come straight to the hall, it seemed, from delivering a load of timber nearby and was still in his working clothes. He was a thin, spare little man whereas his wife was on the large side, and looked even larger in a bright pink coat and matching hat with feathers on it.

In spite of her size, Mrs Hodges was surprisingly fleet of foot and took the last second helping of trifle from under Rebecca's nose. Rebecca then heard her boasting about Nicola's brilliance as a violinist to the mother of one of the budding ballerinas.

'Poor Nicola!' she whispered to Tish.

'Takes all sorts,' Tish whispered back, with a tolerant grin. 'Doesn't seem to have affected Nicola. She seems quite sweet. Look at her now, with Sue, hanging on to every word Sue says. I can't remember looking up to the Second Years like that.'

Rebecca enjoyed the party and began to wonder if she had been imagining things earlier, in thinking there was something up with Tish. But when the party had ended, and all the guests had gone home, Tish said something that was completely out of character.

'I think I'll have an early night,' she said.

'Are you all right?' asked Rebecca, who had been looking forward to the three of them talking for hours, and playing back Tish's cassette recordings from the concert.

'Of course I'm all right,' said Tish. 'Just tired, that's all.'

Now Rebecca was convinced that something was wrong.

She was dragged off to play table tennis by David and Edward and Sue. The Murdoch home even had its own games room. They played good, fast games and worked off the excessive amount of food they had consumed. It was well past her usual bedtime when the party broke up.

'What's the matter with Tish?' asked Rebecca, as Sue led her upstairs and showed her to a little guest bedroom. 'Had a quarrel?'

'Of course not!' said Sue. Then added: 'But she's a bit quirky at the moment, isn't she?'

'Quirky – yes. That's the word.'

But what could she possibly have to be quirky about? wondered Rebecca, as she cleaned her teeth and got ready for bed.

Only Tish Anderson herself knew the answer to that. And she wasn't saying.

TWO
Three Secret Wishes

On the long journey down to Trebizon on Tuesday the three of them spent a lot of time running up and down the train, greeting old friends in other compartments. Then they settled down to a game called 'Confessions', a kind of forfeits game which they played with a pack of cards. If someone drew an ace the others could extract a 'confession' from her, and every word of it had to be true.

'Confess a secret wish to do with school,' said Tish, when Sue drew an ace.

'I can't!' said Sue, blushing. 'You'll laugh at me.'

'You've got to!' said Rebecca. 'It's the rule.' She was expecting Sue to say she would like to play a violin solo at the end-of-term concert, or something similar. So her words were quite a surprise.

'Well,' said Tish gently, 'you'll just have to make do with scoring dozens of goals this term instead.'

As soon as Rebecca drew an ace, Sue decided to get her own back. 'Confess *your* secret wish,' she said, and it was Rebecca's turn to be embarrassed, and the turn of the others to be surprised. Rebecca was especially gifted at writing things, and they expected her to say she wanted to get something in *The Trebizon Journal* again.

'Well, I'd be happy just to be in the Under-14

team,' she said. 'Like you two are. And stay in it. And play in the Gold Cup with you. But that's impossible and I know it is.'

The other two looked at her sympathetically. Rebecca was a fast runner, and a promising hockey player, and was one of a pool of reserves for the Under-14 team. She had played once last term and acquitted herself quite well. But the fact was that the team was full and, amongst the reserves, a First Year girl called Sheila Cummings had already emerged as outstanding and was now the official First Reserve.

'Of course, I could always poison a few of you,' said Rebecca, slightly nettled by their sympathetic looks. They all laughed.

She and Sue were just waiting to pounce on Tish when, at long last, she also drew an ace from the pack.

'Confess *your* secret wish!' they said in unison.

And suddenly she clammed right up.

'I can't,' she said. 'I just can't!'

'But you've got to!' exclaimed Sue.

'Can't.'

'You rotten cheat!' said Rebecca.

'Why did you ask me mine then?' complained Sue. She and Rebecca exchanged glances. Tish

15

being quirky again! Not just quirky but downright infuriating, and not a bit like her usual self.

They ended the game, then, and turned to reading. There was a slightly frosty atmosphere for a while, but it soon thawed when Tish burst out laughing at something in her book.

'Here's a good one for *The J.J.*, Rebecca!' she said. She read it out aloud. 'There really is such a thing as a squirting cucumber. You only have to touch it lightly and it squirts its seeds at you. Sometimes you only have to walk past it for it to squirt you.'

'Not bad,' conceded Rebecca. 'I'll add it to my list.'

'Let's grow one at school and put it in the Staff Room,' said Sue.

The J.J. that Tish referred to was *The Juniper Journal*, a duplicated news-sheet that they produced and sold around the school for five pence a copy. Tish, who was the only person who could type stencils properly, was its editor and Rebecca contributed a weekly piece called 'Did you Know?' consisting of two or three weird and little-known facts. Rebecca had the sort of mind that stored up useless information like a computer.

It was called *The Juniper Journal* because Juniper

House was the junior boarding house at Trebizon, where all First Year and Second Year girls lived. It was a large modern block right in the centre of the main school complex. As the girls got older, they went into smaller boarding houses set in various parts of the grounds. But for the time being, Juniper House was the centre of Rebecca's world, and where everything happened out of school hours.

Juniper House had its own monitors and officers. Tish, for example, had been its Magazine Officer for two terms, in charge of deciding which contributions from the juniors went into the school's famous magazine, *The Trebizon Journal*. This term, a new Magazine Officer would be elected.

But the most important position, officially called Head of Games, was held by Josselyn Vining. Trebizon believed in giving girls a lot of responsibility from an early age, so that head of games picked the teams and ran things with the minimum of interference from Miss Willis, the games mistress. Joss was in charge of junior hockey, netball and swimming but informally she was just called hockey captain, as that was the major winter game. Similarly, the head of games in the summer term would be in charge of junior tennis, swimming and athletics but would simply be called Tennis Captain. It would probably be the same person: Joss Vining!

The train arrived at Trebizon station at three o'clock and coaches took them to the school. As they climbed up out of the old stone town and juddered along the country road, Rebecca felt pleased to see Trebizon Bay in the distance, even though the sea was grey and angry, looking under the low January skies. Then she saw the familiar buildings again, a lovely blend of old and new, through the bare trees in the parkland that surrounded the school. What would her second term at Trebizon have in store for her? she wondered, as the coach turned in through the big entrance gates.

For Tish and Sue, the first thing it had in store was Joss Vining! She was waiting for them on the steps in front of old school, as they got off the coach. A lot of girls had come down on the train from London but many more, like Joss, had been driven from all parts of the country by car.

'Can you get your hockey stuff, you two, and come out on to school pitch right away?' she asked.

During the Christmas holidays the girls were allowed to leave their winter games things in their lockers as they were needed again for the spring term.

'We've only just got here!' exclaimed Tish.

'Sorry, but there's a team practice,' said Joss. Rebecca noticed that Joss, usually the most relaxed of people, looked rather strained. 'We've been drawn in Group Two for the Gold Cup and we've got our first match exactly one week today – against Hillstone. So you see, we've got to get cracking. The trouble with this term is it gets dark after tea and a lot of practice will have to be done over in the sports hall, and that's never the same. In other words, this afternoon is too good to miss!'

'Of course, Joss. You're right as usual.'

Having recovered from their surprise, Tish and Sue agreed with her. On the first day back there was never much to do before tea except wait for the trunks to come up to the dormitories and unpack them. It was a dry afternoon and the pitch was firm.

'I'll take the stuff out of your trunks for you when they come up, if you like,' volunteered Rebecca, 'and that'll give you a bit longer. I'll come down and watch after that, if there's time.'

'You're an angel!' exclaimed Tish. 'Can you get these things upstairs as well?' Immediately Rebecca found dumped in her arms a load of hand luggage, additional to her own. There were two blue school capes, three carrier bags, Sue's violin case –

'Hey!' said Rebecca.

'I'll help!' cried Mara Leonodis, as her brother drove away in his red Mini. She waved goodbye to him.

'Me, too,' said Sally Elphinstone, who was getting off the coach.

'Thanks Mara. Thanks Elf.' Both the Greek girl and plump Sally were in the same dormitory as Rebecca, Tish and Sue. They were a nice group in number six. Rebecca smiled in relief as they took some of her load.

'Okay?' asked Tish, as she and Sue went off with Joss.

'Just about!' said Rebecca.

'But if we're going to wait on you,' called Elf, 'you'd better win the Gold Cup and no excuses.'

Actually, Sally was only too happy to wait on them. She shuddered at the very thought of racing round a hockey pitch as soon as one got back. What a shock to the system! Rebecca, of course, merely envied them.

They trooped through the main school building, which was a converted manor house, out into the quadrangle gardens at the back and across to Juniper

House. Up in the second floor dormitory they dumped everything on to the right beds and then lazed around and chatted. Rebecca knelt up on her bed and gazed out of the window. There was a little copse at the back, with a path leading through it down to the sand dunes and the sea. When the leaves were on the trees you could only catch glimpses of the sea, but now there was a wide view of the bay, with a big tanker on the horizon. It was good to be back.

'They're bringing the trunks up already!' exclaimed Rebecca, as she saw the men with trolleys down in the courtyard below and then heard the thud of footsteps on the stairs.

She unpacked her trunk and put everything away. Then she took all the stuff out of Tish's and Sue's trunks and piled it on to their beds, ready for them to sort it out after tea. Trunks had to be emptied quickly, and stacked on the landing, as the men would be coming back to take them down to the store-room.

'What's that?' asked Mara, as two pieces of paper fluttered on to the floor from the top of the pile on Tish's bed.

Rebecca picked them up.

'Notices about the election of a new Magazine

Officer,' she said. 'Fancy Tish being so tidy-minded and typing them out in the holidays!'

The two notices were identical. One would go on the noticeboard in the First Year Common Room, which was at the opposite end of the building, and the other would go up in the Second Year Common Room, at this end of the building. They said:

Election of Magazine Officer
Having served two terms as Magazine Officer for Juniper House I am calling an open meeting. This will take place at 7 p.m. on Thursday in the Second Year Common Room. According to the school rules a new Magazine Officer must now be elected. She will serve for two terms. As there are two complete terms before anyone moves on from Juniper, this term only Second Years can stand. In the case of a vote, this will be taken on a show of hands.

Ishbel Anderson
Magazine Officer (Retiring)
Juniper House.

'Now I see how Tish got to be elected Magazine Officer when she was still a First Year!' exclaimed Rebecca with interest. 'Every other year an election falls at the beginning of the summer term, when the Second Years aren't going to be in Juniper for two terms, and that's when the First Years get a chance.'

'Rebecca!' said Mara. 'You are better than a pocket calculator. I was never able to work it out before.' The Greek girl shook her head. 'No wonder I am in II Beta when the rest of you are in II Alpha.' But she was smiling broadly.

'Don't think we're going to vote for you, Rebecca,' said Margot Lawrence who had just come in. 'Unless you want us to badly.'

'Eh?' Rebecca was surprised. 'I'm much too new to be anything like that.'

'It's not that,' said Elf. 'If you're Magazine Officer you can only choose other people's stuff for *The Trebizon*. You're automatically disqualified from choosing your own stuff!'

'And we all want that essay of yours to go in this term, the one that Elizabeth Exton kept out,' said Margot. Elizabeth, the former editor of the school magazine had left in disgrace and now there was a proper editor called Audrey Maxwell. 'Bet Audrey will agree.'

Rebecca felt a little rush of pleasure, and said nothing.

'Hey,' said Margot suddenly, 'it's going to be funny Tish not being something important this term. She was a First Year monitor all last year, and then Magazine Officer as well . . .'

'Tish is always important!' said Mara, with great affection. 'And besides, she's still editor-in-chief of *The J.J.* and that's something important!'

'I've got a good joke for it!' remembered Margot. 'Listen to this: How many girls at Caxton High School does it take to put a light bulb in?'

'How many does it –?' giggled Rebecca and the others. Caxton were old rivals and insulting their intelligence was a favourite pastime at Trebizon.

'1001!' said Margot triumphantly. 'One to hold the light bulb in and a thousand to turn the school round.'

They all hiccupped with laughter, and Rebecca had to tear herself away. She wanted to see how the Under-14 practice was going, and if she didn't hurry it would be over. Supposing half the team had gone off form? Supposing . . . Rebecca smiled at herself. What a hope!

There was just enough of the practice left for

Rebecca to see that they were all in great form, especially Judy Sharp who played at right wing, Rebecca's natural position. The forward line was practising running, passing and shooting. Judy went at lightning speed, cracked the ball across to Sue who then in one sweet, deft movement shot it straight past Jenny Brook-Hayes in goal.

'Hurrah!' cried someone on the sidelines. 'Good old Sue!'

It was Nicola Hodges with a crowd of her First Year friends. They seemed to have formed a Sue Murdoch fan club.

Joss blew a whistle then and the practice ended. Nicola remembered Rebecca was at the party at Sue's house and came across to her. Her chubby, angelic face was pink and in spite of a frisky wind her beautifully brushed and plaited flaxen hair was as tidy as ever.

'Wasn't Sue marvellous?' said Nicola.

'Was she?' asked Rebecca. 'I've only just arrived.'

Rebecca was conscious of Joss and Tish standing talking together nearby and she wanted to go over and join them. But Nicola was hanging around, as though anxious to have a long and earnest discussion about Sue. Then suddenly Rebecca realised that Joss was speaking to Tish very privately and had no idea she could be overheard.

'It may not happen, Tish. Don't tell anyone. Promise?'

'Of course I promise, Joss.'

Rebecca turned away quickly. She realised that Nicola had overheard, too. She took the younger girl by the arm.

'So you and your friends are hockey fans, Nicola?'

'Oh, we are now that Juniper's team's got into the Gold Cup!' said Nicola. 'And I've told the others how I've got to know Sue and what a great person she is – so we're going to turn up for every match, you wait and see.'

'Let's go over and talk to Sue then,' said Rebecca.

She was anxious to steer Nicola away. She had the clear impression that the younger girl was more than just interested in the conversation between Joss and Tish.

As they walked across to Sue, Rebecca glanced back over her shoulder. Joss, usually such a calm and relaxed person, was still talking to Tish and looking worried. More mysteries – more secrets! It was bad enough Tish being quirky – now there seemed to be something up with Joss.

THREE
The Team is Picked

Whatever was up with Joss Vining, there were more surprises in store as far as Tish was concerned. On Wednesday the new and unpredictable Tish, whom previously Rebecca had regarded as such a steady person, suddenly seemed hysterically happy about nothing. And, as Rebecca was soon to discover, this new-found euphoria was going to spill out in all directions. Tish, to put it mildly, had hit a high.

They were back into lessons. English came first with their form-mistress, Miss Heath, followed up by a cold douche of mathematics from Miss Gates. She set them a complicated problem to work out in their heads. Rebecca was amazed when four girls, usually the slowest, smugly put their hands up first: Debbie Rickard, Joanna Thompson, Roberta Jones and Mary Bron. Tish started giggling but Rebecca realised nothing until Miss Gates suddenly clapped her hands, later in the lesson.

'Will the four girls who have been given pocket calculators for Christmas and have them on their laps please bring them up here and put them on the table.'

Sheepishly the four trudged up and handed them over.

'You may use your new-found brains in chemistry, physics and biology. I believe the science staff approve. In my lessons you will learn to use your old brains until you are in the Fourth Year. Now, let's continue.'

Sitting in the back row, Tish doubled up with laughter until she started to choke. Judy Sharp, who shared a double desk with her, had to bang her hard on the back. Sue and Rebecca, in the adjacent desk, thought it was funny, too – and soon Tish had all three of them in hysterics.

'Let's go to Moffatt's!' she said at morning break, meaning the school tuck shop. 'I'll buy you lemonades.'

'It's not your birthday,' said Rebecca, in surprise.

At Moffatt's Tish drank her lemonade in one

long draught, gave a contented sigh and leaned back in her chair.

'I think we're going to win the Gold Cup. I just have a feeling about it.'

'Good,' said Sue, humouring her.

'And what did you think about the Head's announcement in Assembly?' added Tish.

'What, about not leaving the taps running in the cloak-room?' asked Sue, puzzled.

Tish let out a shriek of laughter that made several Third Years at the next table turn round in surprise. She shook for some moments.

'What announcement do you mean, Tish?' asked Rebecca patiently.

'The Hilary Camberwell Music Scholarship of course,' said Tish, steadying herself, but with tears of laughter in her eyes. 'Oh, Sue, you are priceless.'

Rebecca remembered the announcement now. It had come somewhere in the middle of a long burble of notices read out by Miss Welbeck, the Principal, in the big assembly hall. *Will all girls entering for the Hilary Camberwell Music Scholarship shortly after half-term please note that the entry forms must be returned, signed by their parents, by January thirtieth.*

'Oh, that,' said Sue.

'It was announced at the end of last term too, wasn't it?' said Rebecca. Her memory for detail, as usual, was good. 'It's for the best instrumentalist under fourteen on September first and it carries up to full fees and free music tuition up the school.'

'Something like that,' said Tish airily. 'But the main thing is that the person who wins it is known as the Music Scholar of her year for the whole time

she's at Trebizon! And they wear those lovely badges with HC on them. We've seen them, Sue!'

'That's right. Moyra Milton's got one. She won it last year,' said Sue. Moyra was a talented clarinet player who was now in the Third Year. 'So what?'

'So *what?*' exclaimed Tish. 'Don't you realise this is your last chance to enter, Sue! Your very last chance. You're only just inside the age limit. Only *just!*'

'Enter?' Sue's mouth fell open in genuine amazement. 'Me?'

'Yes, you!' Tish looked at Sue as though she were a simpleton. 'Who else! You could win it, Sue! Easy!'

'But – but –' Sue looked bewildered, 'I don't see how I could win it for a start. I'd be the oldest,

30

seeing when my birthday is –'

'You could still win it!' interrupted Tish, overflowing with largesse. Rebecca began to feel excited. There was something about Tish's mood today – it was catching!

'And secondly, even if I could win it, well . . .' Sue looked embarrassed, 'it wouldn't be fair. I mean, aren't the scholarships for people who are hard up. My parents don't need me to have a scholarship and –'

'That's got nothing to do with it, Sue!'

'Surely there's a means test or something?'

'Of course not. The honour's the main thing, being known as a Music Scholar all the time you're here. Imagine it, Sue!'

'I think Tish must be right,' said Rebecca. 'Why else would it be *up* to full fees awarded? Parents probably accept the fees if they need them, otherwise they don't. Then there's more money in the kitty for another year.'

'Of course I'm right!' exclaimed Tish. 'Look at Annie Lorrimer!'

'You're right about Annie!' gasped Sue. 'I'd never thought about it before.' Annie Lorrimer was in the Lower Sixth and was also the Music Scholar for her year. 'The Lorrimers are rolling.'

Sue, as a member of the school orchestra, was actually far more conscious of the Music Scholars than Tish had ever been. Their names were all up in gold letters on the honours board, over in the music school. She knew how respected they were, but it had never occurred to her that she could be one, too. Until now.

'There's the bell!' said Tish, jumping up. 'Let's go. It's all decided then!'

There was still a touch of frost on the lawns as she went dancing ahead to old school, back to lessons. Sue and Rebecca followed slowly in her footprints. Rebecca could tell that Sue was inwardly excited.

'What do you think?' asked Rebecca.

'I think Tish is on a high today!' said Sue, trying to keep sensible. 'First of all saying we're going to win the Gold Cup – now this.'

'But it *would* be a nice idea to enter, wouldn't it?'

'Yes,' said Sue. 'If I'm good enough. If I really stand a chance. That's the first thing I've got to find out. I know Mrs Borrelli will tell me honestly. Tish really has no idea.'

'Nor me,' confessed Rebecca. 'But you're right. Mrs Borrelli will know.' She was Sue's violin teacher.

'Is she in today?'

'Yes, I've seen her car.'

'Then you could see her at dinner break, Sue,' said Rebecca.

'You bet!' Sue's spectacles shone as a glimmer of sunlight caught them. 'That's just what I'm going to do!'

'You're late, Susan,' said Mr Douglas, the chemistry master, as Sue came into the science laboratory just after two. Her sandy hair was wind-blown and she had been running.

'I'm sorry, sir, I've been over at the Hilary, and then I had to go and see the school secretary and then I forgot my books –'

Tish and Rebecca, bending over a bunsen burner, nudged each other. Sue forgetting her books? Something exciting must have happened. Sue came and joined them at the long bench and they started whispering together at once.

'What did Mrs Borrelli say?'

'She was surprised at first but, yes!' Sue's face was shining. 'She says I do stand a chance if I work really hard, and she'll put me into the scholarship timetable. Then she asked me if I had my parents' permission and I told her they didn't know anything about it!'

'So what happens now?' hissed Tish.

'I'm going to ring them tonight, but I'm sure they'll agree. I'm so sure I've been and asked for an entry form to be posted off to them today!'

'So that's why you've been to see Mrs Devenshire –' began Rebecca.

'Stop talking!' ordered Mr Douglas. 'Now you've actually got here, Susan, I'd be grateful if you could get on with the experiment.'

The afternoon ended with a double lesson of hockey.

For once Joss Vining didn't play. She stood on the sidelines with Miss Willis, carefully noting form.

So many girls played as forwards that Rebecca often had to be content with a half-back position during lessons. But today, with Joss missing, her chance came. Tish took over as centre-forward in the red team, Judy Sharp moved over to the left inner position, and Rebecca got the chance to play her best position, right wing.

She put everything she had into the game, feeling it just might be important. This feeling grew stronger when she saw Joss walk across to east pitch for ten minutes to watch a game going on amongst the First Years. Her suspicions were confirmed at the end of the lesson. Joss gathered everybody around her on the pitch.

'We had a good Under-14 team last term, but all the same I want to make one or two changes for the Gold Cup. I'll put the names up tonight, with the names of First reserve and Second reserve, who'll travel to matches with us. I'm also going to pick a Second Eleven for this term, which must be willing to play against the Under-14 team at certain times, and give them plenty of practice.'

Miss Willis, who had been keeping in the background, stepped forward.

'It's going to be a taxing term but it could be a

marvellous one,' she said. 'We didn't think we'd qualify for the Gold Cup, but we have. It's a short term and it's going to be packed, because of course we have to fit in our normal fixtures as well. Everyone is going to have to work very hard, keep very fit and be dedicated to the idea that we bring the Gold Cup back to Trebizon for the first time in our history. The girls who will be in the Under-14 team will be expected to give quite a lot to their hockey for a while. Those who are going to be asked to be in the Second Eleven will also have an important role to play. A big burden is going to fall on your head of games this term –' she gave Joss Vining a solicitous glance, '– and I want you all to support her and back her up in every way.'

It was a stirring little speech, and Rebecca felt excited by it, though mildly surprised by that solicitous glance. Joss could look after herself, couldn't she? She was always in complete command, and nobody ever questioned it. That was why she was such a good captain.

'By the weekend I'll have the complete timetable sorted out of fixtures and practice matches up to half-term,' Miss Willis was saying. She laughed. 'I'm booking time on the computer right now! As Joss says, she'll put the teams up tonight. If you're in them – I'm warning you – don't arrange too much for mid-week and weekends this term. I'll see you all again tomorrow. Dismiss.'

They went over to the sports centre to have a shower and change. Now it was Rebecca's turn to be at the receiving end of Tish's new-found euphoria.

'Rebecca! You heard what Joss said?' she asked, as they walked through an avenue of bare chestnut trees towards the main school buildings for tea. 'She's going to make some changes in the team.'

'About time,' Sue said softly.

Suddenly Rebecca was reminded of Sue's funny little confession in the train – her secret ambition to be in charge of the hockey team! Well, Sue had something else to occupy her mind now, something actually within the bounds of possibility. But Rebecca's own secret wish, simply to be *in* the team, burned inside her more strongly than ever. And she knew that Tish was referring to it.

'The changes won't include me,' she said realistically.

'What about the two reserves, though!' exclaimed Tish. 'Sheila Cummings will be one – but I bet you'll be the other! Judy's ankle will never stand the pace.

If two reserves are allowed to travel to matches, one's just got to be a reserve for Judy! And that's you.'

Rebecca had been trying to dismiss the thought from her mind, ever since Joss had mentioned that two reserves would be travelling to all the Cup matches.

It was a fact that Judy had a funny ankle that let her down sometimes. It was also a fact that while some of the other reserves were better all-rounders than Rebecca, she was the one who excelled on the right wing, Judy's position. For the first time, Tish's confidence made Rebecca feel that she really might stand a chance.

'I hope you're right, Tish,' she said.

'I bet I'm right!'

After tea, Rebecca spent the evening in the Second Year Common Room. English prep was to read their set book. Normally Rebecca would have gone to the library in old school, her favourite place. But this evening she sat glued to a chair in the Common Room. She simply had to be there when Joss came and pinned the team list up on the big noticeboard behind the door.

When Joss came in, a crowd appeared. As soon as she had pinned up the list and left the room, they clustered round it. Rebecca walked over, trying hard to look casual.

She saw at once that she was down as right wing for the Second Eleven, but that the two reserves for the Under-14 team were to be Sheila Cummings and Verity Williams, a Second Year girl who was in Form II Beta, and a good defence player. Tish and Sue still had their inside forward positions in the team. That went without saying.

Rebecca bit her lip and went over to the window, gazing out at the lights of the school buildings, twinkling round the quadrangle gardens. How dark and wintry it was outside! Tish and Sue came in a few moments later, looked at the noticeboard and came straight over to her.

'It's not fair, Becky,' said Tish, with feeling.

'It looks as though Joss has decided to take a chance on Judy's ankle, after all,' said Rebecca. 'Rung your parents, Sue?'

'Just been ringing them,' she replied. 'My mother says she's sure Daddy will agree and she'll get him to fill in the form when it arrives tomorrow.' Sue smiled. 'She said it sounded like a great honour, but not to get myself in a stew about it. Oh, Rebecca, it is a shame about you.'

Rebecca glanced at Tish, who was looking sheepish. So much for her euphoria! She had been wrong about the team list. Rebecca hoped she wasn't wrong about Sue's chances, too. Entering for the scholarship was going to mean a lot of hard work for her, especially with all the extra hockey this term. Feeling slightly depressed, Rebecca decided that she liked Tish best when she was just being her normal self.

But she was going to have to wait some time for that.

FOUR
Rebecca Counts Her Blessings

By Thursday afternoon, when it was double hockey again, Rebecca had put her disappointment behind her. Now that the team had been announced, there was a kind of Gold Cup fever in the air, and all the talk was of their first cup match against Hillstone the following Tuesday. To add to the excitement, it was going to take place on the Trebizon ground.

Even without being in the team, or a reserve, it was impossible not to be infected by it. Rebecca began to see that, as a member of the newly-created Second Eleven, she really would have a role to play.

In the interests of the Cup, Miss Willis explained, the First Years and Second Years were going to be mixed up together in the hockey lessons from now on. This was so that on Tuesdays, Wednesdays and

Thursdays, which were the hockey afternoons, the full Under-14 team could have practice matches against the full Second Eleven. Although the Under-14 team itself was mainly made up of Second Year girls, it contained three players from the First Year, and there were several more First Years in the Second Eleven.

Before the first practice match began, on Thursday, Joss Vining gathered her team around her to discuss tactics. Miss Willis drew the Second Eleven over to the other side of the field.

'Play hard,' she told them. 'It really does matter. Not just in this match – every match. You've got to stretch our Juniper team, and keep on stretching them. That way you'll help bring them up to peak form for the cup matches – and keep them there.'

Rebecca, for one, played her hardest and it was an exhilarating game. Mara Leonodis had got into the Second Eleven, too, at right inner, and she and Rebecca discovered that they played very well together. There was a kind of telepathy between them when they occasionally managed to get a run up the field, and short clean passes whizzed backwards and forwards between them as they dodged round the Under-14 defence. It was from one of Rebecca's passes that Mara cracked a goal straight past Jenny Brook-Hayes, the Under-14 keeper.

In reply the Under-14 team scored five good goals, two each from Tish and Sue, and a sheer beauty from the right-winger, Judy. Surprisingly Joss, at centre-forward, did not score. Rebecca noticed she was moving less fluently than usual but it was also a tribute to Verity Williams, playing at centre-half in the Second Eleven, who marked her well. Rebecca decided that Verity fully deserved her selection as Second Reserve for the Gold Cup.

That evening a different kind of selection took place: the choosing of a new Magazine Officer for Juniper House, for two terms. Tish, as retiring Officer, chaired the meeting and the Second Year Common Room was packed out, with a lot of girls standing.

Rebecca was mildly surprised to see Nicola Hodges and her First Year friends sitting in the best chairs, right in the front row. They had obviously arrived very early. But the reason, which she should have guessed, was made clear as soon as Tish asked for nominations.

'I propose Sue Murdoch!' said Nicola, leaping to her feet, flaxen plaits flying. She glanced eagerly across to Sue, who was standing by the door.

'And we second it!' chorused her friends.

Sue went a deep shade of pink and shook her head vigorously.

'I'm sorry, I just couldn't take it on this term,' she said, 'and besides I don't think I'm the right person. I'd like to propose Jenny Brook-Hayes, because I think she would be very good.'

'And I second that!' said Sally Elphinstone promptly.

'Are there any more nominations?' asked Tish.

Rebecca watched Jenny's face and felt for her at that moment. She wanted the job badly, and she would be good at it. Twice she had had something shortlisted for *The Trebizon Journal*, without success, and to have something printed in the school magazine was a cherished ambition. Of course she would have to forego that for another two terms if she were elected Magazine Officer, but it meant she was the sort of person who would not turn down anybody else's work lightly. Everything would be considered very carefully.

'I propose Debbie Rickard,' said Roberta Jones, rather aggressively.

Roberta bitterly resented the way that her

poems, which were awful, were never shortlisted by Juniper House and sent through to the editor of the school magazine, way up in the Upper Sixth. Other people's were. With Debbie as Magazine Officer, things might be different.

'I second that,' said Mary Bron, who secretly thought that the gang in dormitory number six always seemed to have everything their own way.

But Jenny was not kept in suspense for very long. There were no more nominations and Tish took a vote. With Nicola and her friends following Sue's lead and voting for Jenny, and most of the Second Years present doing likewise, Debbie Rickard was defeated by a crushing forty-one votes to seven.

Tish immediately handed over the chair to Jenny and gave her some notes. Jenny studied them and then, cheeks glowing with happiness, stood up.

'Thank you for electing me,' she said. 'I'll keep it brief. Audrey Maxwell, who as you know is the new editor of *The Trebizon*, wants our contributions in by the end of the month. The spring term issue is always a slim one, so I don't think we should send up more than four items. I would like to propose that two of those items should be our two outstanding ones from last term, which Elizabeth

Exton deliberately kept out. The essay by Rebecca Mason and the drawing of the church by Susannah Skelhorn.'

There was a great roar of approval. A crowd of hands shot up and Rebecca felt herself going hot with pleasure. Jenny went on to ask for all contributions to be submitted within ten days, but Rebecca hardly heard her. First a poem in *The Trebizon Journal*, and now a real chance of her essay going in! Margot

Lawrence had hinted at this, on their first day back, and it seemed that her hints were based on solid fact. Rebecca's pleasure was only equalled by that of Susannah Skelhorn, a First Year girl who was an artist of exceptional promise.

'Well,' said Tish after the meeting had broken up, 'that went pretty well, didn't it? Especially the bit about your essay, Bec.'

They were drinking hot chocolate and eating biscuits in the kitchen, opposite the Common Room. Rebecca said nothing, still glowing pleasantly with the memory of it.

'Do you realise, Tish,' said Sue solemnly, 'that for the first time since you got to this place you're nobody important! Just plain Ishbel Anderson. It must feel funny!'

'I like it,' said Tish. She looked at Sue intently. '*You're* the one who's going to be somebody –' She flung up a hand, dramatically. '*Susan Murdoch – Music Scholar!*' she announced loudly to the empty room.

Rebecca and Sue laughed. She was off again! Although not quite as high up in the clouds as she had been the previous day, she was still impossibly good-humoured.

'Put those rose-coloured spectacles away, Tish,' said Sue. 'You haven't really got a clue whether I'll win or not. I've got a long way to go.'

'There's something that might help you,' said Tish mysteriously.

'What?'

'Oh, tell you later.'

'I've just thought of something,' said Rebecca. Actually it was Mara who had said it first, on Tuesday. 'You're still editor of *The J.J.*, so you *are* someone!'

'So I am!'

'Shall we do one this weekend or d'you think it's too early?'

'Of course we'll do one!' exclaimed Tish. 'There's tons of news to put in it already.' She held up her fingers and ticked the items off. 'There's Sue entering for this music thing. We'd better find out who else is, they'll all be in Juniper. There's the Gold Cup match on Tuesday, we can write up a bit about Hillstone's record. The Under-14 team list, of course. The Magazine Meeting tonight, and what was decided. That's four things for a start!'

'I'd better be thinking about my "Did-You-

Knows" then,' said Rebecca.

Later, Rebecca cleaned her teeth and got ready for bed. She came into the dormitory in time to see Tish putting something on Sue's locker, and Sue protesting about it.

'I can't, Tish!'

'Look, Sue, stop arguing. Will it be useful, or won't it? There's a new tape in it, and you know how to work it. You can record when you want and then rub off and start again, until you get it perfect.'

At last Sue gave in. It was a marvellous idea. Tish wanted her to borrow her cassette recorder for as long as she needed it, so that she could record herself practising the violin. It would undoubtedly help her a great deal in the weeks ahead.

But it was noble of Tish to part with her favourite new possession like that! As Rebecca got into bed, she felt quite emotional. She began to feel slightly ashamed of herself, coveting Verity Williams's place on the team list yesterday, thinking she might have been good enough to have it herself. Wasn't it about time she shut her eyes and counted her blessings?

She had found two perfect friends at Trebizon. For all her odd ways lately, Tish was the nicest person she knew – not counting Sue. Everybody had been marvellous about her essay at the magazine meeting tonight. It hardly seemed credible that she might get something published two terms running! And Joss *had* selected her for the Second Eleven – that was quite an honour, too, when you thought about it. She'd only been playing proper hockey for a term . . .

Then there was *The Juniper Journal* . . . it was fun bringing that out each week . . . having a regular piece to write for it.

Rebecca became sleepier and sleepier. The four news items that Tish had outlined and the people concerned became jumbled up in her mind . . . Sue was playing in goal . . . Jenny Brook-Hayes was holding a violin . . . and then she changed to Nicola Hodges. And Rebecca was fast asleep.

The Juniper Journal, in fact, never went to press before Sunday evenings. That was when it was typed and duplicated, ready to be sold around the school on Monday mornings. It was going to be nothing like what they had planned on Thursday night. By Sunday, a lot of the hot news that Tish had been talking about was going to be completely out of date. By then, like the changing images in Rebecca's mind, everything would be upside-down.

FIVE
The First Quarrel

'You've got a letter, Susan,' said Miss Morgan, as the girls trooped downstairs on their way to breakfast on Friday morning. She was the full-time House Mistress in residence at Juniper House and had already sorted out the post. 'Here, read it over breakfast.'

Sue took the stout white envelope eagerly.

'It's from Daddy,' she told Rebecca, looking at the handwriting. 'Posted yesterday, first class mail from London. It'll be the form!'

The bell went for breakfast.

The girls rushed out of Juniper House and along the back terrace which overlooked the quadrangle gardens, to the big modern white building that stood at right angles to Juniper. Girls sat ten to a table in the dining hall and the three friends were on Joss Vining's table, as they had been last term.

'Is that your birth certificate, Sue?' asked Sally Elphinstone, as Sue slit open the envelope with a knife and pulled out the contents. 'Let's see!'

Sue's birth certificate was passed round the table while Sue examined the entry form that her father had completed. There was a brief note attached to the front. She showed it to Rebecca and Tish.

'Daddy's pleased!'

'What does it say? I can't read it,' said Rebecca. Howard Murdoch's handwriting, as was often the case with busy and important people, was almost illegible. 'It looks like "Grrrr hmhh Sue. What a sprrrr squiggle"!'

Tish peered at the note eagerly, and interpreted.

'It says "Good Luck, Sue. What a splendid idea"!'

'What's a splendid idea?' asked Elf, all agog. She handed the birth certificate carefully back to Sue. 'And what's this for?'

'Sue's entering for the Hilary Camberwell Music Scholarship,' said Tish grandly, as though she personally had invented it. 'What's more, she's going to win it –'

'Oh, *Tish* –' protested Sue.

'Hope it's not going to interfere with hockey,' said Joss Vining suddenly, dishing out bacon and sausages from a big casserole. 'How often have you got to practise this term? How much has the orchestra got on?'

Rebecca was surprised by the unaccustomed sharpness in Joss's tone. She looked strained somehow. What *had* she been talking about to Tish the other day?

'Music times have never clashed with anything before,' said Sue, happily. 'I've got my first lesson this evening and Mrs Borrelli's promised to show me the new timetable.'

Sue carefully put the form and birth certificate back in the envelope. She would hand them in to the school secretary immediately before lessons.

'When you go over to the music school this evening,' said Tish, stuffing down the last of her cornflakes, 'find out who else is entering. It can only be people in Juniper because of the age limit, so it'll make a good item for *The J.J.*'

'You bet I will,' said Sue, pushing her spectacles up her nose. 'Never mind *The J.J.* I want to *know*!' She looked at her father's note again, which she had kept beside her plate, and then back to Tish. 'Thanks for the whole idea. I'd never have thought of it myself.'

Rebecca and Tish smiled at one another, and Tish winked. It really looked as though Sue were getting the bit between her teeth! Rebecca dismissed the slight doubts she had had on Wednesday evening. Yes – it was worth Sue trying for an honour like this, even if it did mean extra hard work.

Friday was the only netball afternoon and Joss Vining did not turn up. It was rumoured that she was in the sick room.

'I thought she might be going down with something!' said Rebecca. 'She hasn't looked too good lately.'

'Did you see her at dinner time?' exclaimed Elf.

'She gave me her shepherd's pie; she looked sort of in pain.'

'Enough to give anyone a pain, seeing you wade through a double helping of shepherd's pie, Elf,' said Tish.

Rebecca had the impression that Tish was changing the subject. Then everyone started discussing anxiously whether Joss would be fit for the first cup-tie on Tuesday or not, and Tish said sharply:

'Come on, you lot. Are we playing netball or aren't we?'

After tea that evening, Sue went off to the Hilary in high spirits, taking her violin case with her. The Hilary, short for the Hilary Camberwell Music School, was a group of converted coach houses set by a small lake in the school grounds. It was a beautiful setting in which to learn music. There were a lot of small practice rooms where the girls had tuition in various instruments, and one large room where orchestra rehearsals took place. Trebizon was very strong in music, not least because Hilary Camberwell, a famous old girl of the school, had endowed these buildings as well as the annual music scholarship.

Sue's first violin lesson of the new term with her tutor, Anna Borrelli, went very well. She spoke warmly to Sue at the end.

'I can see you have kept up your playing during the holidays. Good. I am glad that you have decided you will enter for the music scholarship; it will extend you. A high standard is required. You will have to be very dedicated this term.'

'Who decides about the scholarship?' asked Sue, with interest.

'None of the Music School staff have any say in it!' explained Mrs Borrelli, with a laugh. 'That would be quite wrong. Three experts come down from London, and examine you all in turn, and their decision is final.'

'And parents' means don't come into it at all?' asked Sue anxiously.

'Not at all. The Music Scholar is quite simply the most promising young musician in any one year. She will automatically receive free music tuition for the rest of her school career. But the matter of the school fees – that is discretionary. For some people, they are very important. For others, less so.'

Sue nodded. So Tish and Rebecca had been quite correct.

'And who will I be competing against?' asked Sue. 'Am I allowed to know?'

'Of course! There are five of you altogether. You and Nicola Hodges are entering on the violin –'

'Nicola?' exclaimed Sue. She felt suddenly uneasy.

'And three girls on wind instruments. As you go out, you will see the list, and you will also see that a special timetable has been arranged for scholarship candidates this term. Copy all the details down. It's most important that you stick rigidly to the programme we have organised for you. The orchestra also has some important engagements this term, note those down as well, with practice times.'

Mrs Borrelli gave Sue a sheet of paper and a pencil and saw her out of the room. She was expecting her next pupil.

The next pupil was Nicola Hodges.

She came in by the side door, right by Sue. Sue was quickly jotting down the details of her timetable, from the Music School noticeboard. Although Sue had felt buoyant earlier she now felt rather flat, and her brief conversation with Nicola did nothing to help.

'Hello, Sue.'

The two of them looked at the noticeboard

together.

'Timetable's up then,' said the younger girl.

'Looks like we're rivals,' said Sue, awkwardly. There was a long silence. 'When did you enter for it?'

'My parents entered my name for it as soon as I came to Trebizon last term. They'd read about it in the school prospectus.'

Sue looked at Nicola's cherubic face. She could tell the scholarship meant something to the Hodges – perhaps it meant a great deal.

'Nicola!' called Mrs Borrelli, looking out of Room One. 'Are you ready?'

Nicola hurried across to her. Sue folded up her sheet of paper and put it in the pocket of her skirt. Then she walked out of the building and looked at the water. Street lamps illuminated the footpath alongside the lake, which led back to the main school buildings. Their reflections danced on the water.

Sue walked slowly back to school, her violin case hanging rather limply at her side.

Meanwhile, in the Second Year Common Room, there was a slight stir of interest. Miss Willis, the games mistress, had come in and pinned something on the noticeboard. She handed another sheet to Margot Lawrence.

'Margot, be a dear and go and pin this up for the First Years.'

It was the timetable that Miss Willis had promised to have ready by the weekend. She had managed to sort out the complicated tangle of cup matches and regular fixtures, though only after a great deal of telephoning to avoid clashes. And she had also managed to fit in a heavy programme of practice games and training sessions for the Under-14 team.

'Phew!' said Rebecca, gazing at it.

Tish had caught up with Miss Willis by the door.

'How's Joss?' she asked. 'Is she going to be all right?'

'We don't know yet,' said Miss Willis, going out.

'Look at this, Tish!' called Judy Sharp. 'We're going to be worn to a frazzle.'

There were only four of them in the Common Room and they were still discussing the timetable when Sue came in.

'Come and have a look at this, Sue!' said Rebecca.

Sue walked over and gazed at the noticeboard, dully. Then she took a folded sheet of paper out of the pocket of her skirt and smoothed it out.

She looked down at it, then up at the noticeboard, checking back and forth, several times.

'What's the matter?' asked Tish.

'Well, that settles it!' said Sue.

'Settles what?'

'Come on, you two,' said Rebecca, 'let's go and make cocoa.'

They went across the corridor to the kitchen. They had it to themselves and Rebecca started to make three cups of cocoa. Sue had flung herself down at the table, staring at her piece of paper. Tish was craning her neck to get a good look at it.

'It's impossible!' said Sue. 'Look – all the times clash! Either I pull out of the scholarship or I pull out of the hockey team.'

'*Sue!*' said Tish, though Rebecca had already guessed.

'Well, I'm not going to give up my place in the team!' said Sue fiercely. There were tears starting up in her eyes. 'I'm not!'

'But, Sue you'll have to –' began Tish. She was pale.

Rebecca mixed the cocoa to a smooth paste and waited for the milk to boil. She wanted to cry with disappointment for Sue. What a horrible choice to have to make!

'What d'you mean I'll have to?' asked Sue. 'We've got into the Gold Cup!'

'But, Sue, you're being stupid! You've got the rest of your life to play hockey! You'll never ever have the chance of being a Music Scholar at Trebizon again, wearing that badge and having your name up on the honours board –'

'Oh, fiddle the honours board!' said Sue, but Rebecca knew that she didn't mean it. She had only once seen Sue as upset as this before. 'I'm going to pull out of the scholarship.'

'You *can't!*' Tish was angry now, beginning to lose her temper. 'I don't understand you. I thought you'd decided this was really important to you –'

'It is – it was,' said Sue, losing her temper back. 'Except I don't really need it, do I? As a matter of fact other people need it more than I do, people like Nicola Hodges –'

'Is she entering?' asked Tish sharply. 'What's she been saying?'

'She hasn't been saying anything!' retorted Sue. 'I just have a feeling it matters to her, that's all. And it might interest you to know, I feel rather mean.'

'Sue, don't be so utterly stupid,' said Tish.

Rebecca brought the cocoa over to the table. She was keeping out of the quarrel. The trouble was, she could see both points of view equally well, especially now Sue had said that about Nicola Hodges. It could be that Nicola's parents were really hard up! Well, Rebecca's own parents weren't exactly rich. She knew that she was only at Trebizon by courtesy of her father's firm, since they'd posted him overseas.

'Sorry, Rebecca, I don't feel like any cocoa,' said Sue, getting to her feet. 'I'm going up to bed.'

She went out through the door. Tish jumped up to follow her, looking annoyed.

'Come back, Sue. Talk about it properly –'

Rebecca grabbed the back of Tish's jumper and pulled her down into her seat again.

'Leave her alone, Tish!' she said. 'You can't run Sue's life for her. You can see she doesn't want to talk about it any more tonight.'

Tish looked so sorrowful that Rebecca added:

'Cheer up. Let her sleep on it. Maybe she'll see sense by the morning.'

'She'd better.'

That was all Tish said.

But the next morning there were other things to think about. The whole of Juniper House was buzzing with the sensational news. It buzzed along the corridors, through the washrooms and into the dormitories. By breakfast time, there wasn't a girl in the whole of the junior boarding house who didn't know about Joss Vining.

She had been taken to hospital in an ambulance. It seemed that an old back injury, which occasionally gave a little trouble and then quietened down again, was now causing serious pain. Joss's parents had been contacted and a specialist had been to see her. It seemed that a small operation could fix everything – that, and several weeks in hospital.

Afterwards, Joss would be as fit and strong as ever. But in the meantime, she would be absent from Trebizon for the rest of the term.

SIX
Towards a Break-Up

'Cheer up, you lot, she isn't going to die, you know,' said Pippa Fellowes-Walker. Tall and pretty and a member of the Lower Sixth form, Pippa was Rebecca's favourite prefect. The seniors were allowed to wear what they liked at the weekends and Rebecca thought that Pippa looked as good as any model. She wore a flared corduroy skirt with big patch pockets and a russet-coloured polo neck jumper that toned in with her tan skirt. Her golden hair cascaded down over her shoulders. 'Muesli, Rebecca?'

Pippa was one of the prefects on duty in dining hall on Saturday morning. She felt sorry for the kids on Josselyn Vining's table and instead of parading up and down keeping law and order, she had slipped into Joss's old place at the head of the table and started serving out their breakfast to them.

'She's known she might have to have this operation for a long time,' said Tish, who was sitting next to Rebecca. 'She just hoped it wouldn't have to be this term, that's all.'

Rebecca looked at Tish and understood. So *that* was what they had been talking about on the hockey pitch on Tuesday. Joss had made Tish promise not to tell anyone, and Tish had kept her promise.

'But it is!' said Sally Elphinstone,  overhearing. She put into words what was in everybody else's mind. 'How are we going to win the Gold Cup now, without Joss?'

'I don't know,' said Tish, looking determined, 'but we are. Joss will be lying in hospital and just counting on it!'

'Who will be captain?' asked Sue suddenly.

'Goodness knows,' said Pippa. 'Come on, cheer up, shut up and eat up. Doesn't anyone want grilled bacon? What's the matter with you all?'

Towards the end of breakfast the duty mistress rang a small hand-bell, waited for silence, and then made an announcement. Mrs Beal's voice was very firm.

'Miss Willis has requested that *all* First Year and *all* Second Year girls remain seated at their tables when the breakfast things are cleared away. *Even* if you have activities arranged, none of you is to leave the hall before Miss Willis gets here.'

Chairs scraped and voices babbled and crockery clinked as one by one the older girls' tables were cleared away and abandoned. Obediently the First and Second Years remained behind, seated. Their tables were bare and wiped down now and there was a steady murmur of talk. An air of expectancy hung over all the tables. Rebecca, like everybody else, guessed that Miss Willis was going to talk to them about Joss. What was she going to say? Saturday morning was free time and it was very unusual not to be allowed to leave the dining hall. It had to be important.

As the tall games mistress strode in, wearing a blue Trebizon track suit, her short, curly fair hair looked unruly. Sara Willis had not in fact had time to comb it that morning. There was an urgent, business-like air about her and everybody stopped talking at once.

'I wanted to corner you while you're all together,' she said crisply, 'and before the weekend starts in earnest. I expect you all know about Josselyn by now. I've just come back from the hospital.'

There were subdued whispers. Over by the door Pippa Fellowes-Walker and Annie Lorrimer, who was also on duty, hung on to listen to all this.

'Josselyn is in pain, but she is going to be fine,' said Miss Willis. 'I don't have to tell you how upset she is about the Gold Cup, and what a tonic it's going to be for her if we can go ahead and win it just the same. At the moment, Juniper House has no head of games and that means the Under-14 team has no captain. You're like a ship without a rudder and we've got to put that right as quickly as possible.'

Miss Willis's statement caused quite a stir and there was an immediate babble of talk and discussion on the other tables. Rebecca's own table, though, was oddly silent. A ripple of subdued excitement ran round it as they realised, some of them for the first time, what might be coming. Rebecca herself, still recovering from the shock of Joss's sudden departure, hadn't given a thought to the implications.

The games mistress deliberately let the noise run on for a while and then she clapped her hands for silence.

'There's a vacuum and let's fill it as quickly as possible,' she said. 'You all know the procedure for electing a head of games. Names are proposed and seconded and if more than one candidate decides to stand, we organise a ballot. I hope we can avoid that. I hope we can all reach agreement amongst ourselves, right now, on who should step into Josselyn's shoes. I don't have to remind you that our first cup fixture is on Tuesday.'

Tish was looking at Sue, and Sue was looking at Tish. Rebecca's heart was beating very hard. She knew just what Miss Willis was going to say next, and she said it.

'It's between two girls, isn't it? Ishbel Anderson and Susan Murdoch are the only girls who have been in the team as long as Josselyn, from the time they started at Trebizon in fact. Both are outstanding players and have the experience to lead the team this term. And both of them, I know, would have your full support at a difficult time like this.'

There was an almost eerie silence. Then it was broken.

'I propose Sue Murdoch!' shouted Nicola Hodges.

A cheer went up from the First Year table where

Nicola sat.

Sue looked amazed – and then thrilled. She simply could not hide her pleasure.

Debbie Rickard, sitting at the next table to Rebecca, looked across and saw the expression on Tish's face. Tish looked as though she wanted to kill Nicola Hodges! Debbie had always been jealous of Tish and now she could hardly keep the glee out of her voice.

'I second that!' she called out.

There was more applause and murmurs of approval. As Miss Willis had said, there was a vacuum and they all wanted it filled. It would be nice to get it over with at once, and get out and enjoy their Saturday morning, knowing that everything was neatly settled. Sue Murdoch was a fine player, and she was fair; she'd be okay as captain if that's what everyone wanted.

As more discussion broke out Rebecca saw Tish lean over to Sue, with a rather wild look, her black curls almost standing on end. She was mouthing the words, urgently.

'The music scholarship, Sue! *The music scholarship.*'

'I'm pulling out of that, Tish. *I told you that last night.*'

69

Miss Willis raised her voice above the babble. She was looking directly at Sue.

'Would you be willing to stand, Susan?'

'Yes,' said Sue.

'Is everyone content to leave it at that –?' began Miss Willis.

Suddenly Rebecca felt Tish's fingers gripping her arm, so tightly that it hurt. She whispered into Rebecca's ear. Sue saw, and so did some of the others.

'You've *got* to propose *me*,' she said.

'Tish –' began Rebecca, shocked.

'Please, *please* trust me.'

That was all she said. Rebecca didn't stop to think. It was all mad. Everything about Tish was mad this term.

But she did trust her. She would have trusted her with her life.

'I propose Ishbel Anderson,' she said, voice shaking a little.

Mara Leonodis, who sat at the same table as Debbie Rickard, was waiting to release her pent-up feelings. Of *course* Tish should be the new head of games. And Rebecca thought so, too! That was good enough for Mara.

'I second!' she cried.

There were some cheers now, and two whole tables applauded. Tish Anderson was very popular.

Miss Willis waited for the din to cease, and then she smiled.

'Now, which one of you is willing to stand down?' She said the words confidently. She knew that the two girls were best friends, and that they were both very sensible, and that they would hardly want to force an election over the issue.

There was silence, and her voice faltered a little.

'I'm sure one of you is?'

Sue stared at Tish, an expression of hurt disbelief on her face. Then she looked down at the table, resolutely.

Tish, equally resolute, sat with her arms folded,

staring into space.

'Are there any more nominations?' asked Miss Willis.

There weren't.

'And Ishbel and Susan are both certain they want to stand?' asked Miss Willis. She stared at both of them, in turn. Both nodded their heads, very slightly, and said nothing. Everything was still in the dining hall. 'I see.' There was a hint of irritation in her voice. 'Then we shall have to organise a proper election,' she said. 'But we can't do anything over the weekend.'

She turned and saw the two prefects, who had been listening with great interest.

'You two,' she said briskly, 'organise a ballot in Juniper House on Monday evening. I suggest directly after tea. Ask Joanne to be there when the votes are counted.'

Joanne Hissup was in the Upper Sixth and was head of games of the entire school. It made the whole thing seem very important.

'Well,' said Miss Willis, turning back to the seated girls, 'with a bit of luck Juniper House will have a new head of games by Monday evening, and as we are meeting Hillstone on Tuesday, that won't be a moment too soon. I want the election to be conducted in a good atmosphere, with everybody pulling behind the new captain when she has been elected, and may the best girl win. You may go.'

Without a backward glance at Tish or Sue, she strode out of the hall. Pandemonium broke out as the girls scraped their chairs back, gabbling loudly as they left the dining hall in groups, discussing this extraordinary turn of events.

Tish Anderson and Sue Murdoch fighting each other for Joss Vining's old job! They were supposed to be best friends weren't they? It was Rebecca Mason's fault – that new girl who went around with them. What was she trying to do, stir up trouble between them?

'Tish Anderson *asked* Rebecca to propose her,' chipped in Nicola Hodges there. 'I saw her!'

'You didn't!'

'What a thing to do!'

'But Tish *would* be best!' said someone else. 'She always scores more goals than Sue!'

And so the argument and discussion raged on.

Tish went up to Sue and touched her on the shoulder, about to say something. But Sue angrily shook her off and marched out of the hall. Rebecca could see that she was on the verge of tears.

Tish started to follow her and then stopped. Nicola had caught up with Sue on the terrace outside, and was talking to her animatedly. They were joined by a crowd of Nicola's friends.

Mara Leonodis and some other girls mobbed round Tish, pledging their support.

Debbie Rickard came up to Rebecca and said sweetly:

'I suppose if Tish is elected you're hoping to get in the team?'

Rebecca felt sick, at that. She felt even sicker when she heard a First Year girl say to her friend:

'Do you know what Nicola Hodges thinks? She says Tish Anderson will go to any lengths to get it, even if it means breaking up with her best friend.'

'Miss Willis wants the election to be conducted in a good atmosphere,' thought Rebecca. 'Some hopes of that!'

She had put Tish's name forward because she had begged her to. Tish had asked Rebecca to trust her, and Rebecca had complied. But Tish was baffling this term, she really was. Why did it all matter so much, anyway? And now people were starting to say horrible things. Hadn't Tish realised that they might?

Rebecca hovered by the glass doors of the dining hall. Sue was still on the terrace, surrounded by supporters. Rebecca longed to go out there and say something, but the look that Sue gave her chilled her to the bone. It was full of reproach. She quickly turned her face away.

There was Tish in the hall, talking to Mara, Sally and Margot. Tish looked quite sparkling, the light of battle in her eyes. She was sitting on one of the long dining tables swinging her legs.

Had Tish no idea how upset Sue was? Could she really be that insensitive? Had she forgotten about Sue's secret ambition to be a hockey captain – just for a term? Joss would get fit and well again, thank goodness, and she would be head of games all the way up the school. Everyone knew that. This was the only chance Sue would ever have.

Tish wasn't bothered about being anything this term. So why was she spoiling things for Sue? It could only be because she had this fixation about the Music Scholar business. Sue's name in gold letters on the honours board and all that. But Sue didn't want it! She had been excited at first, but she had soon changed her mind, when she had realised it was going to interfere with her hockey. Sue had already been planning to drop out of the Hilary Camberwell!

'Doesn't Tish realise, thought Rebecca fiercely, that this is going to break the three of us up? I've got to stop her. The whole idea of having an election is idiotic and I've got to stop it before it even starts.'

And then Mara called her over.

SEVEN
The Election is On

'Rebecca! You were marvellous!' Mara's large brown eyes were shining as she looked from Rebecca to Tish and then back to Rebecca. 'You were the only one of us who had the courage to do the right thing!'

'Tish made me,' said Rebecca. 'You all know she did!'

'And she was right!' said Margot.

The little group was quite alone in the vast dining hall now.

'Do you notice something, Rebecca?' asked Tish. 'The Action Committee has reactivated itself. Great minds thinking alike again.'

Subtly, Tish was reminding Rebecca of the events of last term. At that time, when there had been a clash with the mighty Elizabeth Exton over an injustice towards Rebecca, Tish had formed a little 'Action Committee'. It had consisted of herself, Sue, Mara, Margot and Sally 'Elf' Elphinstone and it had helped to win the battle against Elizabeth.

But Rebecca was in no mood for nostalgia.

'It's not quite the same committee this time, is it?' she said coolly. 'There's someone missing.'

'That's right,' said Tish, outrageously calm. 'Sue's missing. We're all going to gang up on her and stop her being daft. Are you going to join us?'

'No, I'm not!' Rebecca said furiously. The words poured out and she couldn't stop them. 'I don't know what's got into you this term, Tish. I don't know why you asked me to propose you just now, and heaven only knows why I did it! I must have been mad! You've taken it into your head to run Sue's life for her. *You've* made up your mind that she's going to be the Music Scholar this year, when she doesn't even want to be any more –'

'That's only part of it,' said Tish hastily.

'Then what's the rest of it?' asked Rebecca. Tish being baffling again! 'Whatever it is, it's not worth it. Do you realise people are already starting to say nasty things about you –'

'So what, as long as they're not true.'

'And about me,' added Rebecca.

'Are they?' Tish was taken aback.

'But the worst thing is *Sue*. We've made her utterly miserable. She was so amazed and thrilled when it looked as though she was going to be given Joss's job, and she just can't understand what you're up to. She's hurt, Tish. *Please* drop it – just drop the whole thing.'

There was so much emotion in Rebecca's voice that the others were embarrassed and silent. She hadn't intended to say so much. Tish looked upset and for a moment Rebecca thought she might have won the day. But when Tish finally spoke, her hopes were crushed.

'Not a chance,' she said. 'Of course Sue was amazed and thrilled, as you put it. Amazed, especially. It had just been a daydream of hers. She's not cut out to run things while Joss is away, especially not to win the Gold Cup. She's not aggressive enough. You can see it when she plays. She's clever and skilful and she makes a lot of goals for other people, but she doesn't go crashing through and scoring them. Another thing is, she can't take too much pressure. She gets uptight. Her mother's always telling her off about it.'

'And you wouldn't,' said Rebecca scornfully. Did Tish really believe all that stuff? 'Stop electioneering, for heaven's sake!'

'Me?' said Tish, unabashed. 'I'd be okay. I've got more will to win than Sue has. Take the Hilary Camberwell.' A note of rebuke crept into her voice. 'One look from Nicola Hodges and Sue wants to back down.'

'*That* girl has the will to win all right,' said Mara Leonodis darkly. 'Who stuffed the idea into Sue's head that she should be a busy little hockey captain? What a strange coincidence, hey?'

'Oh, I don't think Nicola planned that,' said Tish quickly. 'She's not the sort. She looks a sweet, innocent sort of girl to me. The trouble is she worships the ground Sue walks on and it goes to Sue's head. The main thing now is to nip this whole thing in the bud.'

'You've got to win the election on Monday, Tish,' said Margot Lawrence. 'Aren't we supposed to be going over to Moffatt's to plan out our campaign?'

'I haven't just got to win,' said Tish calmly. 'I've got to crush her. Nothing else will do.'

'*Why?*' asked Rebecca, aghast. 'Why do you have to do *that*?'

'So she'll realise, once and for all, that the whole idea was silly. Then maybe she'll get down to what really matters, working hard for the Hilary Camberwell.'

'That she *can* win,' said Mara. Mara herself had a lovely singing voice and, unlike Tish and Rebecca, a good musical ear.

'You really think so, Mara?' asked Tish.

'I know it!' said Mara and added, under her breath: 'And so does Nicola Hodges.'

'Oh, come off it, Mara!' For the first time that morning Tish's grin was back in place, huge and irrepressible. 'I'm sure you're wrong about Nicola.' She slid down off the table, ready to go, and turned to Rebecca. The others were already walking towards the doors. 'You won't join us then?'

'Tish,' said Rebecca, close to despair, 'maybe you'd do the job better than Sue, maybe you wouldn't. But none of it matters. If the election goes ahead, it's going to break us three up. Please call it off. Anything's better than you two fighting each other.'

'It won't break us up,' said Tish. Rebecca was amazed. She sounded so sure, so confident. She grabbed hold of Rebecca's arm, and lowered her voice. The others were over by the door, waiting for her. 'I asked you to trust me before, and you've got to go on trusting me. I don't want this election, any more than you do. I tried to talk to Sue earlier, but she wouldn't listen. She might listen to you. If you really want to make yourself useful, go and find her. Try and get it into her thick head that I care about her and I'm trying to stop her doing something she'll regret . . .'

'Come on, Tish!' called Elf. 'I'm starving.'

'And tell her to drop out of the contest!' finished Tish. 'Coming, Elf!' she called. 'How can you be starving? You've only just had breakfast!'

Rebecca watched as they all went outside. A few snowflakes were falling and some landed and shimmered briefly on the back of Tish's dark curly head. She heard their voices going off into the distance, across quadrangle gardens.

She came out and shut the doors carefully behind her. She stood on the terrace, uncertain, undecided. Then she made up her mind.

'I believe you, Tish,' she thought. 'Thousands wouldn't. I still don't know what you're really up to, and why it all matters so much. But whatever it is, I don't think you're doing it for yourself.'

For the second time that morning she found herself doing Tish Anderson's bidding. She set off to find Sue Murdoch.

'Tish has put you up to this, hasn't she?' said Sue, furiously. 'Of course I'm not going to drop out of the contest! Why should I?'

Rebecca's heart sank.

She had tracked Sue down to one of the small practice rooms at the Hilary. She had glimpsed her through an open door, head bent over her violin, playing a haunting piece of music. She had waited outside for her to finish the piece, somehow comforted by the sounds. Sue was not ignoring her timetable then.

That was the beginning and end of any comfort that Rebecca Mason was going to receive from Sue Murdoch that morning.

'Don't get so angry, Sue,' begged Rebecca. The cold glint of the eyes behind the spectacles was almost more than she could bear. 'Tish honestly believes she's doing you a favour. She thinks you'd make a mess of Joss's job and you'd kick yourself for ever more, when you looked back and saw what you'd given up.'

'She does, does she?' said Sue. 'Of course, it couldn't possibly be that she wants to be head of games herself –'

'Sue!'

Rebecca was shaken.

She had naturally expected Sue to be hopping mad with Tish for interfering in her life and trying to decide what was good for her. Who wouldn't be? She was also waiting to be mowed down in a hail of verbal bullets for putting Tish's name up for captain.

But this – It was completely unexpected.

'Tish is a hypocrite!' Sue burst out.

'Sue . . .'

'I'm sorry, but it's true.' A look of utter incomprehension came across the sandy-haired girl's face. Rebecca realised that, beneath the anger, she was on the verge of tears. 'She knew all along that Joss might be going!'

'What do you mean, Sue? What are you driving at?'

'Look, Rebecca, do I have to spell it out? Tish is quirky when we see her in the holidays. Why? She's suddenly realised she's coming back to school this term without a job to come to! She feels lost. She's a born organiser, is Tish! She loves to be at the centre of things – in charge –'

'Oh, Sue!' Rebecca laughed out loud. Could this really be Sue talking? 'Of course she does, but –'

'Don't laugh. Just listen. As soon as she gets back to school she finds out that Joss is in a bad way and someone may have to take her place –'

'Hey!' said Rebecca. But Sue would not be silenced.

'And suddenly she's up in the clouds! You remember! Says we're going to win the Gold Cup! Suddenly becomes wildly interested in Hilary Camberwell Music Scholars, badges, names up in gold, me playing the violin all hours of the day and night. Tish! Who hardly knows one end of a violin from the other! Be honest, Rebecca. Has Tish ever taken the slightest interest in the Hilary Camberwell Music Scholarship before? Has she ever mentioned it? Did she even notice when Miss Welbeck explained all about it at the end of last term?'

Rebecca shook her head.

'No,' she agreed. 'She hasn't. She didn't.'

'And suddenly – she acts as though my life depended on it. It all fits together, doesn't it. Admit it, Rebecca.'

'It fits together fine,' said Rebecca, slowly. 'It's just –'

'If only she'd *said*, right at the beginning!' interrupted Sue. 'If she'd just had the guts to admit that she wanted to take Joss's place, I wouldn't have dreamt of standing against her! I'd have backed her up all the way. That's the silly thing about it. But all this stuff about the scholarship! Shunting me off here –' Sue gave her violin case a small kick – 'getting me out of the way! The hypocrite!'

Sue fell silent, tearful and angry. Rebecca felt bemused. How damning the evidence against Tish looked, when Sue spelt it out like that!

'It all fits together fine,' repeated Rebecca, finding her voice at last. 'Except I don't believe a word of it. Not one single word. I know Tish has been behaving mysteriously, and I still don't really know what goes on in her mind, but I'm sure it's not the sort of things you're describing. I trust her, Sue, so why can't you?'

Sue looked at Rebecca reproachfully.

'You're on her side. You want her to win. You haven't been listening to a word I've said. Well you're wasting your time if you think I'm going to drop out of the contest, I've got a lot of support.'

There was a light in Sue's eyes. 'I'm going to beat her, after this. It would give me great pleasure.'

'I'm not on anybody's side,' said Rebecca quietly. 'How did you find out that Tish knew about Joss long before the rest of us?'

'I – I –' For a moment Sue was thrown into confusion. She looked embarrassed. And then she snapped her fingers. 'Tish said so. At breakfast. I heard her say so, to you.'

'True,' said Rebecca, thoughtfully. 'She did mention it.'

Sue picked up her violin and bow, ready to continue. She was anxious to bring the discussion to an end. Rebecca made one last attempt.

'Sue,' she pleaded. 'I'm *not* on Tish's side. I proposed her because she made me. But I'm sure she thinks she's acting for the best. What you've been suggesting is rubbish and I think when you cool down a bit, you'll see it is. I'm not on *anybody's* side. I just want you two to stop fighting each other. Can't you drop out? It's still not too late.'

'No,' said Sue. 'Why should I?' Pointedly she drew the bow across the strings and started to play. Rebecca walked to the door.

'The election's on then?' she said, dolefully.

'The election is on.'

When Tish went up to the dormitory at midday, there was something standing on her bedside locker. It was the smart little cassette recorder in the blue case that she had lent Sue on Thursday. Sue had returned it, without a word, and Tish knew that Rebecca had failed.

EIGHT
A Dirty Election

Rebecca realised it was going to be a dirty election from the moment the first posters went up, late on Saturday afternoon. She saw them when she came back to Juniper after playing hockey.

Now that the election was inevitable, the First Years were throwing themselves into it with gusto. They were split into two camps and there was no limit to their zeal. It was no holds barred! What really shook her, though, were the tactics adopted by Tish Anderson. It was going to be just one more surprise in a long line of surprises; yet another sign that something peculiar had got into Tish this term.

The hockey game lacked excitement. It was the second of the practice matches ordered by Miss Willis, between the Under-14 team and the newly-formed Second Eleven. The atmosphere between Tish and Sue did not help, and the team was conscious of it. They were also missing Joss badly. It had been decided to try Sheila Cummings, the First Reserve and a good all-round player, in Joss's position – centre-forward. But she really didn't compare. The game was a dull affair.

The only exciting thing that happened was the sudden appearance of Mr Barrington on school pitch at the end of the game. He was the Director of Music at Trebizon, always impeccably dressed, and he looked most out of place as he walked to the touchline on tiptoe, trying not to get his shoes muddy.

'Susan!' he admonished. 'You were supposed to be at orchestra practice. This is no way for a potential Music Scholar to behave.'

'I may be voted head of games, sir, now Josselyn's in hospital,' said Sue. 'If I am, I won't be entering for the Hilary Camberwell and I'll be getting written permission to drop out of the orchestra this term as well.'

'Head of games?' Mr Barrington shook his head. 'Tcchh! Tcchh! Anybody can be head of games.'

He went away, still shaking his head, looking

...al as he stepped from one dry patch to the next. Everybody was grinning – except Tish.

When Rebecca got back to the junior house, the posters were starting to appear. Sue's supporters had taken over the First Year Hobbies Room and were turning them out at speed; Tish's supporters had moved into the Second Year's Hobbies Room and were doing likewise.

Some were quite innocuous like VOTE X MURDOCH, with crossed hockey sticks forming the 'X'. Others were less than friendly. SUE WHO? screamed a poster stuck to the door of the television room and, halfway up west staircase, another one said STOP TISH ANDERSON!

At tea time Sue asked the duty mistress if she could change tables. She did a swap with Mara Leonodis who sat on the next-door table, and everyone on Joss Vining's old table could breathe freely again. There had been an atmosphere you could have cut with a knife.

'Though I don't know why it had to be *Sue* to go,' observed Judy Sharp as she doled out pieces of ham from a large plate. She had taken over Josselyn's place as head of table.

'One of us had to,' said Tish blandly. 'Sue's with

her friend Debbie Rickard now.'

Several girls giggled. Sure enough, at the next table, Debbie Rickard was fussing around Sue like a mother hen. Rebecca lowered her eyes. Nobody liked Debbie Rickard, including Sue. It wasn't her fault that Debbie had been the person to support her nomination this morning. Tish was using anything to gain support!

That evening the poster war hotted up. Two awful caricatures were pinned up; one showed Sue with her spectacles dropping off and the other showed Tish with legs like tree trunks. Her legs *were* thick and muscular compared to the rest of her, and Rebecca knew the picture must have hurt. Even more hurtful was the slogan under the picture of Sue: BUT CAN SHE SEE THE BALL?

The two rival camps also started scribbling on each other's posters. To the slogan VOTE FOR SUE were added the words IF YOU HAVEN'T GOT A CLUE, and beneath the simple exhortation TISH! was written something equally horrid.

The First Years were having the time of their lives, until Miss Morgan toured the building and took all the posters down except for four respectable ones. Rebecca felt miserable. Her long hair felt lank and greasy and she could feel a spot coming up on her chin. She shampooed her hair and gave it a conditioner, bathed her spot, blow-dried her hair and went to bed early.

Her suspicions that Tish would stoop to anything to gain support were confirmed on Sunday.

After church, Rebecca spent the morning in the library composing the 'Did You Know?' piece that she wrote regularly for *The Juniper Journal*. Sunday was its press day, and it was a relief to have something to take her mind off the election.

As this was to be the first issue of term, she wanted to make her piece really good. She decided to write about the squirting cucumber that Tish and Sue had laughed about on the train journey down (how long ago that seemed! But Tish had been rather odd, even then -) and three other useless facts that she selected from the recesses of her mind. Her favourite was the one about the Gimyak tribe in Siberia. *Did you know*, she wrote, *that Siberian Gimyak women have the longest fingers in the world? They are often eight or nine inches long* . . . She had no idea where she had read that, but with Rebecca it was a case of once read, never forgotten.

'You're a walking data bank of useless

information!' laughed Judy, when Rebecca showed her the piece over Sunday dinner. 'It's a good batch this week. Even better than usual!'

But when Rebecca took the piece along to *The J.J.'s* 'publishing office' during the afternoon she received a rebuff. The 'publishing office' was simply a large table in the corner of the Second Year Hobbies Room. On it stood a typewriter, on which were typed out the stencil skins, and next to it a small duplicating machine on which the news-sheets were run off. There was a small crowd of Tish's supporters gathered round it, with Tish in the centre, and there was excitement in the air.

'Sorry, Rebecca,' said Tish, 'but there just won't be room for it in *The J.J.* this week. Hold it over until next week.'

'No room –?' began Rebecca.

'*Election Special!*' said Tish crisply. 'Just a short run this week, to be sold around Juniper. To help everyone make their minds up!' She looked across to Mara Leonodis, who was carefully composing something in an exercise book at a small table nearby. 'How's it coming along, Mara?'

'Fine, Tish.'

Rebecca immediately felt suspicious. She felt

even more suspicious when Debbie Rickard walked into the Hobbies Room at that moment, looking incredibly self-important. She was holding a sheet of paper.

'I've written the article, don't forget to put my name on it.'

As she handed it over, Rebecca caught sight of the heading: 'Why I supported Sue Murdoch for Head of Games – by Deborah Rickard.'

'Don't you dare cheat, Tish Anderson,' said Debbie. 'Don't you dare forget to put it in. And Mara's piece about you has got to be exactly the same length, remember?'

'Of course I won't forget to put it in!' said Tish, glancing at the paper she had been handed. She kept a very deadpan expression. 'What's more I'll run Mara's piece first, and yours underneath. That way you have the last word – what could be fairer than that?'

'Hmmm,' said Debbie. She was obviously worried at the back of her mind that there could be some catch. 'Don't you change a single word!'

'Of course not!' and Tish. 'I'll try not to make any typing errors, either.'

'Has Sue agreed to this?' blurted out Rebecca.

'Of course she has,' said Debbie importantly, and went out of the room. Rebecca followed her out, thinking: 'Poor Sue! I suppose she just didn't have any choice, now Tish has dreamt this up.'

She stood outside in the corridor for a few moments, watching Debbie go up east staircase. She felt suddenly angry with Tish. Nobody liked Debbie Rickard, and Tish knew it. If she were after the floating voters, this was certainly the way to get them! Whatever Debbie had written for the *Election Special* it was bound to be nauseating – and bound to put people off voting for Sue.

She heard subdued laughter coming from inside the Hobbies Room and feared the worst.

By breakfast time on Monday morning, the special election edition of *The J.J.* was already in circulation. And it certainly did nothing to help Sue's cause, as Rebecca had rightly guessed.

The first article was entitled 'Why I supported T. Anderson for Head of Games – by Mara Leonodis'. The writing was not inspired, but it was sensible and factual, listing Tish's good record as a member of the Under-14 hockey team for the past two seasons, especially with regard to the number of goals she had scored. It pointed out that she had natural leadership qualities and had excelled when given responsibilty, first as a monitor in the First Year and latterly as the Magazine Officer for the whole of Juniper House. It did not denigrate Sue in any way.

Debbie Rickard's article came after it, and contrasted badly. It gave very little factual information about Sue, or what her qualifications were for being made head of games this term, but contained some silly and rather spiteful remarks about Tish. It was also most unfortunate that there was a typing error in the very first sentence so that the article began: *Sue Murdoch is very good at playing hookey* . . . This soon became the standing joke of the moment and made Sue seem slightly ridiculous. Rebecca was quite sure that the so-called error had been deliberate.

She looked across at Sue's face, pale and drawn, in Assembly that morning and her heart went out to her.

'No wonder she thinks Tish is just out for herself, and that's all there is to it. It looks more and more like that, all the time. I know Tish thinks that, for her own good, Sue's got to be crushed – but she doesn't have to fight a dirty election!'

All along Rebecca had been baffled by Tish.

Now, just for a moment, as she looked at Sue's face, she came very close to disillusionment. Could Sue be right? Was Tish a hypocrite?

And then she caught sight of Tish looking at Sue. Tish's face was completely unguarded. There was no grin there, just an expression of great anxiety and with it a certain affection. In spite of everything, Rebecca's trust in Tish came rushing back and she felt ashamed for having doubted her.

Monday was the only day when they did not have games – just a whole lot of lessons to slog through. First lesson was English with the form-mistress and Sue asked Miss Heath if she could come and sit in the front. She changed places with one of the Nathan twins, and so Rebecca found that she and Sue were no longer sitting together. It somehow seemed to make the break-up complete.

The election took place immediately after tea. Pippa Fellowes-Walker and Annie Lorrimer organised it very well. They took over the Second Year Hobbies Room, which was the largest room in Juniper House, and set up a ballot box. For half an hour, girls filed in and recorded their votes on special slips of paper, put them in the box, had their names ticked off the register and then left.

Rebecca did not vote. Instead, she stayed in the Common Room and did her geography prep, which was to read about the wool trade. Not a single word of it sank in. For company she had several members of the Under-14 team, who were not voting either. Most of them found the idea of having to choose between Tish or Sue rather distasteful.

'Not voting, Rebecca?' asked Jenny Brook-Hayes, who was the team's goalkeeper. 'But you started the whole thing.'

Rebecca just went on staring at her book.

But they all went down when the result was due

to be announced. The Hobbies Room was packed and girls overflowed into the corridor. Joanne Hissup, as requested, had come over specially from Parkinson House to supervise the count and make the announcement. Rebecca's hands felt rather clammy as Joanne stood up, with a piece of paper in her hand. The room went so still that they could hear the clock on the wall ticking.

'Here is the result,' she said. 'There were nineteen abstentions. Susan Murdoch – twenty-three votes. Ishbel Anderson – seventy-six votes.'

A tremendous roar went up. A crowd of girls mobbed round Tish. The senior girls smiled and pushed their way out of the room.

'Well, that's settled,' said Joanne. 'And Miss Willis will be relieved. Now they can get themselves organised for the Gold Cup. They've got their first match tomorrow afternoon!'

Rebecca saw a small group round Sue, with Nicola Hodges prominent amongst them. Sue looked utterly crushed. Nicola was looking flustered for once. Sue spoke just one sentence, and Rebecca overheard it:

'I blame myself most, Nicola, but let's face it – I look a real fool, don't I?'

It had dawned upon both Sue and Rebecca at the same moment. The result had been a foregone conclusion, right from the beginning. Although – to those who knew her – Sue was well-liked in Juniper House, some girls hardly knew who she was. Tish was universally popular, in a way that Sue could never be. Tish had had no need to resort to her dirty tricks. She would have won the election by a wide margin in any case.

Which only made it all the odder.

'Speech!' shouted someone.

Tish stood up on a chair, giving her widest smile. Her black curls were full of bounce. She waited for the noise to die down.

'Not so much a speech,' she said, 'more just a couple of quick sentences. First, thanks for electing me. Second, I've got to rearrange the team now we've lost Joss – and if you'll leave me in peace with the typewriter for half an hour, I'll sort it out. I'll pin the list up in both Common Rooms straight after.'

There was some clapping and then the meeting broke up. Girls went out chattering happily. The rank-and-file of Juniper House had enjoyed the election, but they were glad that it was over now. Someone was in charge of the hockey team again.

It was nice that it had all been so decisive, with the obvious person emerging as captain. They could forget all about it now, and let's hope they did well in the Gold Cup! Soon, the large room was almost empty.

Rebecca hovered. She had to decide whether or not to congratulate Tish. It was a bit difficult with Sue standing there. Tish was seated at the typewriter now, frowning as she fed in a sheet of paper. Then slowly, very slowly, Sue walked across to her.

'I'll say one thing, Tish,' she said, awkwardly. 'You've proved your point. Nobody wanted me as head of games except for a few infants and lunatics. They all wanted you. I have to hand that to you. I allowed myself to get carried away. Nicola told me I had a lot of support, and I believed her.'

It was all so humbling for Sue. It was taking a lot of courage on her part. To Rebecca's amazement, Tish waved her away.

'Sorry, Sue. I must concentrate on this.'

Sue looked as though she had been slapped in the face. She turned on her heel and walked out of the room. Rebecca followed soon after, seething with indignation. What was the matter with Tish? In spite of what Sue believed to be totally selfish behaviour on Tish's part, she had been trying to make it up. She had been trying to say that the result was right and she accepted Tish as captain.

Tish had got what she wanted, hadn't she? Surely she could relax a bit now?

But Rebecca was not thinking clearly enough. She should have guessed what was coming next.

NINE
Right Out On a Limb

The first Rebecca knew about it was when Sue came rushing into the dormitory, half an hour later, with the tears streaming down her cheeks. It was not yet bedtime, but Rebecca had sneaked up there to try and read her geography book. She just hadn't wanted to be in the Common Room when Tish came in to pin up the team list. It might look as though she were hoping to be on it, when, obviously, she couldn't possibly be.

'Sue!' exclaimed Rebecca, dropping her book on the floor and jumping off her bed. 'Whatever's wrong?'

She ran round her cubicle and along to Sue's, but Sue was already pulling her curtain across with a savage wrench. Girls hardly ever bothered to pull their curtains across.

'Sue,' said Rebecca through the curtain. 'What –'

'Go away!' sobbed Sue. 'You've got my place in the team, isn't that enough!' And she flung herself face downwards on her bed.

Rebecca gasped. She turned and ran out of the dormitory, took the stairs two at a time to the floor below, and walked into the Second Year Common Room. There was an icy silence as she came in. Several members of the Under-14 team were clustered round the noticeboard but now, as Rebecca walked in, they all walked out.

'What a rotten trick!' said someone.

'Winning the election must have gone to her head!' said another. 'It's the meanest thing I've ever seen.'

'But it's not like Tish!' said Jenny Brook-Hayes.

Rebecca stared at the sheet on the noticeboard, going hot and then cold. She had been left completely alone in the Common Room, as though she suffered from the plague. This is what she read:

Under-14 Team List
Trebizon U-14 v. Hillstone U-15
Tuesday 2.30 p.m.

Home

This is match One in Group Two in the West of England Junior Gold Cup and the team and reserves are as follows:

G.K. J. Brook-Hayes

R.B. J. Thompson L.B. R. Jones

R.H. E. Keating C.H. S. Cummings L.H. W. Gorski

R.W. J. Sharp R.I. R. Mason C.F. I. Anderson (Capt.)

L.I. L. Wilkins L.W. M. Spar

1st Reserve V. Williams *2nd Reserve* S. Murdoch

(Signed) *Ishbel Anderson*
Head of Games: Juniper House

So it was true! She had been given Sue's place in the team.

Rebecca looked for a long time and then she went and slumped in a chair, over by the big window overlooking the school quadrangle. Its gardens were shadowy in the darkness. Most of the lights were out in old building, across the way. She could just make out the silhouette of the sundial, set in the centre of the lawns. The building she was in was itself ablaze with light, glowing out into the darkness and lighting up the terrace below. Nobody would be going to sleep early in Juniper House tonight.

For a long time Rebecca had wanted to be in the team. If that wish would ever come true, she used to think, how she would jump for joy! Now it actually had come true, a less joyful sight than Rebecca Mason in that chair would be hard to imagine.

'You look as though you've just been to a funeral,' said Tish, coming in and shutting the door.

'How do you expect me to look?' asked Rebecca, still slumped. 'What do you think you're doing?'

'Making the best of a bad job, of course,' said Tish, in her most matter-of-fact tone. She seemed completely confident that what she was doing was right. She paced up and down the long carpet, enumerating on her fingers as she talked, a favourite habit of hers.

'For a start, I'm the best centre-forward now we haven't got Joss so I've moved over from left inner. I've switched Laura Wilkins to left inner from centre half – I think she'd be good in the forward line. I've put Sheila Cummings at centre half, she's good all round and is wasted as First Reserve –'

Rebecca wasn't listening to any of this, which she agreed with anyway.

'– and I've put you in, instead of Sue. Otherwise the team is just as Joss had it.'

'You've put *me* in – oh, Tish, I like the casual way you say it.'

'You mean you weren't even a reserve and Verity Williams was?' asked Tish. 'But she's a defence player –'

'I mean you've dropped Sue!' yelled Rebecca.

'Of course I have!' snapped Tish. She looked at Rebecca in despair. Why didn't she understand? 'What did you expect me to do, once I was captain? Have you seen the timetable over at the Hilary –?'

'No,' said Rebecca, wearily. 'It's none of my business.'

'Mrs Borrelli started Sue on her first scholarship

piece on Friday,' said Tish. 'She's supposed to practise it every day, and two hours tomorrow afternoon instead of games. If she doesn't know it by Friday she can't go on to her next piece. Do you realise, Becky, she's got to know *four* new pieces for the scholarship and she's only got six weeks to learn them in?' Tish sounded so strange! 'There's no way she can play against Hillstone tomorrow. I've only put her down as Second Reserve so that it doesn't look too awful. The whole team can break their legs, but she's not going to play.'

'It looks awful already,' said Rebecca. She was still completely mystified by Tish. 'Can't you get it into your head that Sue doesn't want to be a Music Scholar? She did at first, but not any more. I know you think it's important for her, and you're probably right. She can play hockey for ever more, whereas this chance will never come again. It *is* a distinction.' Rebecca had been taking note of the Music Scholars in the past two days, the proud way they wore their badges. She had found out about all the special opportunities they were given to develop as musicians, higher up the school. She sighed. 'Yes, Tish, I know all the arguments. But the fact is that Sue isn't interested and you just can't force her to be.'

'I can't force her, but I can persuade her,' said Tish. 'She hates me at the moment. I've just been up in the dormitory trying to talk to her, and she won't listen to a word I say. But give her twenty-four hours to cool down, and she'll listen. Somehow –' there was a look of utter determination on Tish's face '– somehow I *will* get it through to her that everything I'm doing is for her own good. She'll buckle down all right then.'

'You sound very sure,' said Rebecca.

'I am very sure. We've been such close friends, she's always listened to me before.' A bewildered expression crossed Tish's face, as though she couldn't understand why Sue hadn't been listening this time. 'She's always trusted me before, too. Once I make her see . . . once she accepts she's out of the team, and I'm not going to let her in, she'll start trying hard for the Hilary Camberwell because it'll be the only thing she has left.'

'And even if Sue wants to run her own life, and run it quite differently, nothing will shift you?'

'Nothing,' said Tish, with passion.

Rebecca shook her head, helplessly. She started on a new tack.

'The team's taken it very badly,' she said.

'I know,' said Tish, and she looked worried for the first time. 'I can't hope to make them understand. But you understand, don't you, Rebecca?'

'No,' said Rebecca, a lump coming to her throat. 'I'm afraid I don't, Tish. But the funny thing is I trust you.' It was true. She trusted her more than ever now, for the simple reason that she was so burning with passion over the whole thing that somehow she must have right on her side! Also, she was prepared to go right out on a limb. 'You realise, Tish, that some people think you're just being nasty.'

'Of course I realise. And I didn't want to put you in the team, either, because a lot of it will rub off on you. It's just that, with Joss and Sue out, you happen to be the very best person we have now to put in the forward line, after Laura Wilkins.' Tish looked Rebecca straight in the eye. 'If you want to chicken out, just say so. I'll understand.'

For all her dismay at the events of the past few minutes, Rebecca felt a sudden surge of elation. *The very best person we have now* . . . Tish had said it, and she had meant it.

'Chicken out?' she said. 'Not me.'

The atmosphere in the dormitory was fraught

that night. There was Sue's cubicle, curtained off in silent reproach. There were Jenny and Joanna, both members of the team, and also occupants of dormitory number six, glaring at Rebecca and Tish as they came in. Even the other three occupants of the dormitory, Margot and Elf and Mara, all staunch Tish Anderson loyalists, were dreadfully subdued.

Rebecca tossed and turned and woke up several times during the night. Tomorrow she was playing in the Gold Cup in Sue Murdoch's place. Sue was the better player and everybody knew it! Every move she made would be watched, every mistake noted! This was their first match in Group Two and if they lost it they could be on their way out of the Cup! She didn't want to play. She was terrified.

She was up and dressed early. She knelt on her bed by the window and gazed through the bare trees behind Juniper House, to the sand dunes and sea beyond. And she saw that Sue Murdoch had got up even earlier.

She was walking slowly back from the direction of the sand dunes with a companion. The companion was Nicola Hodges. They had obviously been for an early morning walk along the seashore together. They were in deep and earnest conversation. An orange winter sun was rising over Trebizon Bay.

Poor Sue, thought Rebecca. After all she had suffered at Tish's hands, it must be a relief to turn to someone like Nicola Hodges who appeared to offer the unfailing devotion one would normally expect from a faithful spaniel.

'That Nicola!' sniffed Mara Leonodis, who had silently appeared at Rebecca's shoulder. 'That Nicola Hodges girl, she gives me the creeps. She is at the root of all the trouble, you mark my words.'

'What on earth do you mean?'

'I don't know what I mean, Rebecca,' said Mara. 'I just go by instinct in this life. All I know is that there has been nothing but trouble between Tish and Sue since that girl appeared on the scene.'

'Oh, Mara. You're just being silly,' said Rebecca.

She watched them. Sue was putting an arm round the younger girl's shoulders now, as though to comfort her. 'At least,' thought Rebecca, 'I suppose Mara is just being silly.'

TEN
A Visit to the Hilary

Juniper House had talked about it half the night. Tish Anderson and Sue Murdoch were enemies now! Tish had dropped Sue, the star of the team, and put Rebecca Mason in, in her place! By the morning, Tish Anderson's stock had suddenly fallen very low.

'Let's boycott the match!' Nicola Hodges said to the First Years, and Debbie Rickard took up the same cry amongst the Seconds.

'Nobody will listen to them,' Tish told Rebecca.

'I think they will,' she replied.

Miss Willis was already in a bad temper, even before Tish told her (by way of explanation) that Sue's schedule for the next few weeks was going to clash with her being a regular member of the team.

'I had no idea she was even a candidate for the Hilary Camberwell, until Mr Barrington told me last night,' frowned the games mistress. 'He was annoyed that she intended to withdraw if she were made head of games this term – and now I daresay he's pleased. This is all very sudden! There are plenty of suitable candidates for Music Scholar without Susan deciding to add herself to that number. You apart, she's our strongest player.'

At dinner time Rebecca was issued with her own official team sweater which had TREBIZON in large white letters on a blue background. She had played for the team once before, as a last minute substitute when Judy Sharp's ankle had swollen up. But this was more like the real thing, and the sweater proved it. At half-past two she would run out on to the pitch with the rest of the team, wearing that sweater. 'The stuff of my dreams,' thought Rebecca, with bitter humour. As each minute passed, she dreaded the match more.

As dreams went, this turned out to be a very bad one.

The whole of Juniper House had been let off games, to be able to come and cheer. But the whole of Juniper House did not turn up. Not even half of it. Not even a quarter of it. Hillstone, who had brought two coachloads all of fifty miles, had more supporters lining the pitch than Trebizon, the home team!

Miss Willis was annoyed. 'I suppose they think that without Josselyn and Susan we haven't a chance,' she thought. 'What the dickens are they all doing? Watching TV?'

Tish looked round the thinly-lined pitch and was shaken rigid. But she was made of stern stuff. When the starting whistle blew, she just put her head down and stick down for the bully-off, got possession and streaked away. If everybody could have played like Tish, they would have won.

They lost, and for one small mercy Rebecca could be grateful. The rest of the team played as badly as she did! They were all hopelessly out of touch with each other and they just couldn't get going. Again and again Tish tried to get them working together as a team, but they just wouldn't gel. Hillstone won the match by three goals to nil.

'What a mess!' Miss Willis shouted at them, afterwards. 'Call yourself a hockey team. You're on your way out of the cup, before you've even started!' She was angry and disappointed. Trebizon was the youngest team to have qualified for the Gold Cup. On last term's form, she had felt excited about their prospects. 'We're down to play three more matches in our Group. But if you get another result like this against Caxton High next week, you might as well quit!'

'The new forward line's got to come together –' began Tish.

'If there hadn't been an election the team could have been settled on Saturday morning!' said Miss Willis sharply. 'Not late last night. You would have had three whole days to come together, as you put it –'

She stopped. The team was dejected and exhausted. They had played their hardest, they

had run themselves into the ground, and they had nothing to show for it. Now they all seemed to be glaring at Tish, as if everything were her fault. Miss Willis sensed an undercurrent of bad feeling. She didn't want that. She didn't want Ishbel Anderson to be made a scapegoat.

'I'm sorry,' she said. 'The election was your business, not mine. I'm sure it was quite right to hold one, with both Ishbel and Susan keen to do the job. But now it's all settled, for heaven's sake make it work. Now go and get cleaned up and changed and take those miserable looks off your faces, or you'll put the Hillstone girls off their tea. Miss Morgan's organised quite a spread, and she suggests five o'clock. You know what you have to do, Ishbel?'

Tish nodded. As captain of the home team she would be acting as hostess at the hockey tea. Hockey teas took place at the boarding house, instead of in the dining hall, and they were always something special!

'Pass them lots of grub and be terribly polite and see that our lot don't pinch all the best cakes,' said Tish.

The others laughed. That sounded a bit more like the Tish they knew and loved. Even Rebecca raised a smile.

But Tish didn't exactly rush to get back to Juniper House. She was still stuck in a changing room, long after the two teams had showered and dressed and left the sports centre. Rebecca was getting fed up with waiting for her.

'Come on, Tish,' she opened the door and looked in, 'what –' Tish was sitting on the bench. She had obviously been dressed for some time. She was just sitting there, staring into space, a picture of dejection. 'Oh, poor Tish,' she said, and came and sat next to her. 'Cheer up.'

Tish buried her face in her hands.

'Do you think Sue's over at the Hilary?' she said. 'Do you think she's bothering? Because if she isn't I might just as well go and shoot myself!'

Rebecca put an arm round Tish's shoulders.

'Why don't we go and see?' she said. 'And isn't it about time you two got on speaking terms again?'

'You're right.' Tish got to her feet. Some of her old certainty was coming back. 'Perhaps she's stopped hating me and is ready to listen. The sooner that happens the better. Come on!'

She grabbed Rebecca's hand and they ran out of the big white building and along the winding footpath that led to the Hilary. As they came out of the shrubbery and around the little lake, they saw Nicola Hodges come out of the side door of the building, carrying her violin case. She passed quite close to them.

'Hello, Nicola. Is Sue in there?' asked Tish.

'Yes,' said Nicola. There was a wary expression on her face.

'She's ubiquitous!' thought Rebecca. 'She's always around Sue!' Then she chided herself. If Sue had been told to do two hours' violin practice this afternoon then, obviously, so had Nicola. And, as for the other times, who could blame Sue for going round with Nicola? Tish drove her to despair so what else was she supposed to do with herself?

'That kid just worships Sue, doesn't she?' said Tish ruefully, when Nicola had passed out of earshot. 'That's why she got the First Years to boycott the match. I must say, I could have done without that.'

'Come on,' said Rebecca. 'Let's find Sue.'

Tish was worried that the building seemed very silent and she couldn't hear a violin playing anywhere.

They found Sue in practice room number four. She wasn't playing but was standing over by the window, looking out across the little lake. She had obviously been trying to work, because there was some music up on the stand. But her violin and bow lay discarded on a table, with a sealed envelope lying beside it.

'How's it going, Sue?' asked Tish.

'It's not,' said Sue, without turning round. 'And how did the match go?'

'We lost three-nil.'

There was something so utterly despondent in Tish's tone that Sue turned round then. 'I'm sorry,' she said simply. 'I really am. And it wasn't my idea that they should all boycott the match. That was stupid.'

'You don't have ideas like that,' said Tish.

It was clear to Rebecca that Sue had stopped hating Tish. She seemed to have something bigger on her mind. 'What do you want?' she asked.

'I just want to tell you what you wouldn't let me tell you last night. Everything I've done has been so you can forget about hockey this term and settle down and win the Hilary Camberwell music scholarship. Okay?'

'That's your theory,' said Sue.

'It isn't a theory, Sue!' Rebecca burst out. 'It's a fact!'

'Whatever it is, it's all been a waste of time!' snapped Sue. She was very tense and irritable. She walked over to the table and picked up the white envelope. 'I've just written this. It's formal notice in writing that I'm pulling out of the scholarship.'

Tish then behaved in a really amazing manner. She lunged at Sue and grabbed the envelope from her hand, shouting furiously all the time. 'What do you think you're playing at! I haven't gone through all this for nothing! You're going to win that thing, you *are*!' She ripped the letter to pieces and flung it up in the air before Sue could stop her. 'There!'

'Tish!' Sue stared at her in amazement. 'You *do* mean it. It hasn't just been an act . . .'

Tish had slumped into a chair, breathing heavily, spent by her furious outburst and trying to recover. It was left to Rebecca to speak.

'Of course it hasn't been an act, Sue! Tish is obsessed about it! She's put herself out on a limb over this. The whole team's turned against her – as well as most of Juniper. Or hadn't you noticed? She may be nuts, but she isn't acting!'

'Tish.' Sue stared at her friend, and her lips were starting to tremble. 'You really are a stubborn pig. I *told* you I'd gone off the idea, once I found out I'd be competing against Nicola.'

'Nicola?' Tish was very alert again. She gathered all her wits together. Then she spoke fast and compellingly. 'I know how you feel, Sue. I'm sure Nicola's a very nice kid, and maybe the money would be useful to her parents. But you can't back down because of that, and she shouldn't expect you to –'

'She doesn't –' began Sue.

'A competition's a competition,' said Tish fiercely, 'and the best person has got to win. I think Mr Barrington thinks you're the best person, as a matter of fact, but the experts from London will decide that. Nicola's got to take her chance, fair and square. The Music Scholar's got to be the *best* person, that's the whole idea, otherwise the whole thing's a farce . . .'

'Tish!' Sue was trying to break in. Rebecca could see that she was becoming very distressed.

'And look at it this way, Sue, if you do win it won't be a disaster for Nicola. She'll be young enough to enter again next year, but this is your last chance.' Tish got up and went and gripped Sue's arm. 'Your very last chance.'

There was silence. At last Sue spoke.

'I'd worked all that out for myself, Tish. I woke up early this morning and went up for a long walk along the beach. I realised that my dream of stepping into Joss's shoes had all been a total fantasy. I wasn't cut out for the job. It was you they wanted. And that I might as well try for something that I actually am cut out for, Nicola or no Nicola –'

'Then?' Tish's eyes were wide with hope for a moment. She looked at the floor and saw the torn-up pieces of the letter lying there. Her voice faltered. 'Then why did you write out your notice?'

'I met Nicola on the beach,' said Sue.

'And –'

'I can't really tell you. It's not my secret. She didn't mean to tell me. It just came out in a kind of rush.'

'You'd *better* tell me,' said Tish.

'Okay.' Sue took a deep breath. 'You may as well know. If Nicola doesn't win the Hilary Camberwell she'll have to leave Trebizon. You won't tell anyone?' She looked at Rebecca. 'Nor you?'

'No, I won't tell anyone,' said Rebecca. 'Are we allowed to know why? It's money presumably.'

'Yes,' said Sue. 'Her parents knew it was going to be a struggle to send her here, but her mother works as a manageress in a shop and her salary has been paying the fees.' Rebecca nodded. She could just imagine Mrs Hodges in charge of a shop, probably a dress shop. 'Well, just before Christmas they discovered she's got a serious illness and she's had to give up work. So you see –' She spread out her hands in an expressive gesture, '– the scholarship means absolutely everything to Nicola.'

'Yes, I see,' said Rebecca.

Sue bent down and picked up the pieces of torn letter from the carpet and looked at Tish. Tish had not spoken a word.

'There wasn't much point in tearing this up, you know. I've only got to write it out again.'

Still Tish said nothing and Rebecca realised it was because she was dumbfounded. She seemed to be in a state of shock.

'Poor Tish,' thought Rebecca. 'This really is the end of a dream. She's taking it very hard.'

And suddenly Annie Lorrimer appeared in the doorway, arms akimbo.

'Tish Anderson!' exclaimed the duty prefect. 'I've been sent to look for you! They're waiting to start the hockey tea, and they can't start without you! Come on!'

She took Tish by the arm and started to haul her out of the room. The cheerful prefect was never angry with anyone for very long. 'Okay, so you lost the match! What are you doing skulking over here!' Tish was staring, mesmerised, at the lovely mother-of-pearl badge on Annie's jumper with the monogram HC – the badge that only Music Scholars were allowed to wear. She was very close to tears.

Rebecca was left behind, forgotten. She knew she should be at the tea too, but she wanted to stay and talk.

'Poor Sue,' she said. 'You've ended up with nothing you wanted. And we've probably lost the Gold Cup. As for Tish . . .'

'Poor Nicola,' said Sue.

'Is her mother very ill?'

'Yes. It's a serious form of diabetes. She's always been a diabetic, but just before Christmas it got much worse.'

'I won't say a word –' began Rebecca. She stopped. A certain part of her brain started ticking over and sending out signals. It was that curious little bit of Rebecca's brain that stored up useless information. This was to be its big day.

ELEVEN
The Big Showdown

'I totally misjudged Tish, didn't I?' Sue was saying.

'Yes,' said Rebecca. And all the time that word *diabetes* kept going round and round in her brain. 'And she has to take insulin every day? Mrs Hodges I mean.'

'Yes! And lots of tablets as well. Isn't it terrible!'

'Awful,' said Rebecca. 'Only I think it might not be true,' she thought.

'But you must admit she's quirky this term,' said Sue. 'Tish. She's really got me baffled. I don't feel I know her any more . . .'

'True,' said Rebecca, but her thoughts were elsewhere.

The tea bell went in the far distance, over in the main block.

'I'd better dash!' exclaimed Sue. 'And you, Rebecca – you're supposed to be at the hockey tea!' She hurriedly gathered up her music and rolled it up and put it with the violin and bow in the case. The walked across the grounds to the main school buildings and drew apart near the dining hall.

'Who do you have to give your notice to?' asked Rebecca, suddenly, pulling Sue back. 'Don't you have to tell your parents first?'

'I'm writing a letter to them tonight,' said Sue. 'They'll understand.' She was irritable but she tried to hide it. She knew her parents were going to be disappointed. But it couldn't be helped. 'And I give my notice in to Mrs Devenshire. I've missed the office now. I'll write it out again tonight and hand it in first thing in the morning. Hadn't you better hurry, Rebecca?'

But Rebecca didn't go to the hockey tea. Even if she'd felt hungry, which she didn't, she would never have had the nerve to walk in so late. And besides – she had urgent things to do. She hurried over to the school library in old building, got out a large encyclopaedia and checked through it.

She was right, of course she was right! If you suffered from diabetes then you had to be very careful indeed about eating sugary things. But at that party at Sue's house, Mrs Hodges had been stuffing herself silly with cakes and trifles. Rebecca could picture her now, in the bright pink coat, whipping the last helping of trifle from right under her nose.

Diabetes?

Rebecca put the book back on the shelf. She was trembling a little. What to do now? She thought of Nicola with her flaxen hair and her round cherubic face, looking as though butter wouldn't melt in her mouth. But she had to find out more – she had to be sure!

How could she find out about Mr Hodges? She remembered the battered old lorry he had brought to the party with *Hodges Road Haulage* on the side. He obviously worked hard – he'd come straight from a delivery job! Was that one lorry the extent of his business, or were there more? Suddenly she remembered that Annie Lorrimer's father was in road haulage – in a big way. She'd seen the lorries around London, with the word *Lorrimers* on the side, and an arrow symbol. Would Annie know anything?

She found the prefect making her own tea over in Willoughby, the Lower Sixth boarding house.

She had to screw up all her courage to ask.

'Know the Hodges? Yes, of course we do. They live down the road. What's all this about, Rebecca?'

'I just wanted to know – I mean, do you happen to know if he makes a lot of money?'

'Really!' Annie looked shocked. 'What's that got to do with you? It's none of my business, and it's certainly none of yours, Rebecca. What are you doing over here, anyway? You're supposed to be at the hockey tea!'

'Perhaps she wants to touch Nicola for a loan,' said an amused voice. Pippa Fellowes-Walker had just come in. But she noted the fraught expression on Rebecca's face. As Rebecca walked out of Willoughby, dejected, half a minute later, a hand touched her shoulder. Pippa was right behind her.

'What's going on, Rebecca?'

'I wasn't just being nosey!' Rebecca blurted out. 'I've just got to know whether Nicola's parents are rich or not and whether her mother used to be manageress of a shop!'

Pippa was marvellous. She didn't find that in the least extraordinary. She didn't ask questions. 'Leave it to me,' she said. 'You're too late for the hockey tea. Go and get yourself something to eat at Moffatt's.

I'll see you there in a few minutes.'

Rebecca sat in the school shop drinking endless cups of tea. She still didn't feel hungry. Would Pippa never come? The place was empty. Then, at last, a tall and elegant silhouette appeared against the frosted glass panel of the door and Pippa entered.

'Well?' asked Rebecca, very pent up.

'They're rolling,' said Pippa. 'And I gather Mrs Hodges has never done a day's work in her life. In fact, Brian Hodges and John Lorrimer are business rivals –'

'You would never think it to look at him!' exclaimed Rebecca.

'Annie says he goes around looking like a tramp and keeps all his money under the bed!' laughed Pippa. 'And he works day and night as though he's right on the brink of poverty, but actually he owns a lot of lorries and half of Tottenham as well.'

'Well, I'll be blowed,' said Rebecca.

'It's something to do with the music scholarship, isn't it?' said Pippa shrewdly. 'Annie says Mrs Hodges is the most awful woman, who's always boasting and trying to keep up with the Joneses. Because Annie came to Trebizon then *naturally* Nicola had to come here. And four years ago, when Mrs Hodges heard that Annie had been elected the Music Scholar for her year, she started Nicola on the violin the very same week! Now's she told half of Tottenham that Nicola's going to be this year's Music Scholar. Poor kid!'

'Hmm,' said Rebecca.

'Has she been telling your friend Sue a hard luck story?'

'Something like that.'

'I must go, Rebecca, I'm on library duty,' said Pippa. 'Whatever was on your mind, it's nice to see some colour's come back to your cheeks!'

The colour in Rebecca's cheeks, although Pippa did not know it, was caused by blazing hot anger. She sat there, outraged. Poor kid, indeed! As she pieced together the events of the past week, step by step, it occurred to her that Nicola Hodges wasn't devoted to Sue at all. It had all been a pretence. Those angelic looks, the flaxen hair and the baby-blue eyes, concealed a clever, calculating little personality. The only person Nicola Hodges was devoted to was herself.

She must have been nervous about Sue from the start. Violinists were given preference in the scholarship. Rebecca had read that somewhere.

Nicola was the only girl entering on violin this year, the other three played wind instruments. But was Sue Murdoch going to put in for it? She had managed to get friendly with Sue in the holidays, and had reassured herself that she was safe. The scholarship hadn't entered Sue's head!

And then that idiot Tish Anderson had *put* the idea into her head – made her really keen! From that moment on, Nicola had tried every trick in the book to steer Sue into other paths. She had even proposed her for Magazine Officer, last Thursday evening! On Friday evening she had looked at Sue with those big blue eyes of hers and made her feel mean for entering. *That* was the moment when Sue went off the idea, Rebecca decided; the hockey timetable was merely an additional sore. 'That settles it,' Sue had said. Her mind had been made up already. The hockey timetable, on its own, would never have settled it. Sue would probably have decided to put the scholarship first.

But Nicola was still nervous. On the first day of term she'd got wind of the fact that there was something wrong with Joss. Rebecca had been with her when they'd heard Joss and Tish talking about it, on school pitch. Tish was the natural person to step into Joss's shoes – and that would give her the power to drop Sue from the hockey team and persuade her, all over again, to put the music thing first. Nicola was ready for that. On Saturday morning, when Miss Willis raised the subject in dining hall, she jumped in straight away with the proposal that Sue would be the new head of games!

She'd been able at the same time to poison Sue's mind against Tish, by pointing out that Tish had already known about Joss and hence the sudden enthusiasm for Sue to be a Music Scholar! But Tish had won the election, and Nicola was back to square one. Sue had been dropped from the team and her thoughts were going back to the music scholarship – so Nicola had played her last card, this ridiculous story about her mother's illness.

'And just to clinch things, she's been stirring up trouble all day – getting people to boycott the match – so all the pressure's going to be on Tish to put Sue back in the team,' realised Rebecca. It was incredible, all right.

'You let your tea get cold!' said Mrs Moffatt, as Rebecca suddenly got to her feet. Rebecca glanced back at it. So she had! Then she ran out of the tuck shop and over to Juniper House. She took the stairs two at a time, up to the dormitory.

'A cool customer, Nicola,' she thought. 'She's not going to be easy to pin down. But I'm going to settle this!'

She took something small out of Tish's locker and slipped it in her pocket. 'Tell Tish I've borrowed this,' she said to Mara, who was staring gloomily out of the window at the dusk gathering over Trebizon Bay.

'I wonder if Sue will draw her curtains round again tonight?' sighed the Greek girl. 'It is all so terrible, this bad atmosphere.'

'Clever Mara!' observed Rebecca, rushing out of the dormitory.

'Me – clever?' said Mara, but the door had slammed. What on earth was Rebecca talking about?

Downstairs, Rebecca pounced on Nicola. She had just got back from tea. She pushed her along the corridor and into the small television room. Then she shut the door. They were alone.

'You've been telling Sue a lot of lies haven't you!' she said to the startled Nicola. 'You've told her your mother's very ill and had to give up her job. I've checked up, and I know that not a word of it is true.'

Nicola's mind worked quickly. Where had Rebecca got this from? It couldn't have been from Sue. She had sworn Sue to secrecy! Rebecca must have overheard something.

'Surely Sue hasn't told you that?' she asked, her eyes wide and innocent. 'I told her my mother hasn't been very well lately, and that's perfectly true.' She didn't like the expression on Rebecca's face. It was grim! She burst out petulantly: 'It doesn't matter to Sue whether she wins the Hilary Camberwell or not.'

'She can decide that,' said Rebecca. 'You go and find her right now and confess to her about all the lies you've been telling –'

'I shan't!' Nicola stamped her foot. 'I want to be chosen as Music Scholar, my mother's *counting* on it! I'm not going to confess anything. I haven't been telling any lies! Sue didn't even know about the scholarship until that stupid Tish Anderson –'

'Stop it,' shouted Rebecca. She walked across and shook Nicola hard. 'That's for being a liar! And thank you for breaking up my two best friends!'

She took something out of her pocket and held it up.

'I know every word you've said to Sue!'

Nicola gasped, her senses still shaken. Rebecca was holding up a small cassette. Tish Anderson had a cassette recorder, she'd seen it! They must have planted it somewhere today, and left it running. At the Hilary, perhaps? She'd had so many conversations with Sue, she couldn't remember where they'd all taken place. Now it was all on tape . . .

'You shouldn't be allowed to enter at all!' said Rebecca. 'You should be made to withdraw at once. I've a good mind to hand this cassette over to Mr Barrington and get it played through –'

'No!' Nicola dived at Rebecca, who sidestepped. The younger girl stumbled against the wall. Coolly Rebecca put the cassette back in her pocket. Nicola turned round, tears streaming down her cheeks. 'No, *please! Please* don't do that. I'll do anything –'

'Just go and find Sue then,' said Rebecca. 'I expect she's writing her letter of withdrawal right now. Stop her. Tell her the truth – why you wanted her to have Joss's job – why you turned her against Tish – everything.'

As Nicola walked to the door, with leaden footsteps, Rebecca felt a twinge of pity for her.

'If you're going to win, it's better that you win fairly. If you're not going to win, it'll teach your mother not to go round boasting about you! Next time she starts, you can tell her to shut up.'

The members of the Hillstone hockey team were on the coach, ready to start the long journey back. It had been a delicious tea, and records had been played afterwards, but they weren't very impressed with Trebizon's captain.

'Did you ever see such a misery?' said one girl. 'She was supposed to be cheerful and act as hostess. She didn't even seem to want to talk to us.'

'Just because we beat them!'

'The rest of the team thought she was a bit off. You could tell.'

'One of them didn't even bother to turn up – the fair-haired one. Wonder what happened to her?'

Tish stood in the cobbled yard at the back of Juniper House, seeing the coach off. She watched it draw away. She hadn't even the strength to wave. What a mess she'd made of her duties as head of games. If only Joss were back. Calm, happy Joss – she'd have put the visitors at their ease, everything would have gone smoothly. Joss! What was she going to think, lying in hospital, when she heard that they'd lost the match three-nil? Of course, it would be all right to put Sue back in the team now. Except it was probably too late to make any difference to the cup. Everything had been in vain. Everything was a mess . . .

She turned to walk back into Juniper, curls damped down by the fine, drizzling rain. Somebody was waiting for her in the lighted doorway, arms outstretched. 'Oh, Tish! You poor thing!' There were tears of emotion in Sue's eyes. 'Tish . . . I've been so stupid it isn't true! *You're* the one who's been bothering about me, all along. Not – not Nicola –

she was out for herself . . .'

'Nicola was?' asked Tish in amazement. 'But her mother . . .'

'It was all lies. Rebecca found out. Rebecca made her confess.'

'Lies?'

'So I am going to enter, after all. The minute I sat down and tried to write to my parents, and imagined their faces, I *knew* you'd got it right. From the beginning. But there just didn't seem any choice. And then Nicola walked in, looking like a sick cat.' Anger crossed Sue's face. 'Oh, Tish, she's been the most incredible little two-faced hypocrite and I was completely taken in by her! I began to believe awful things about you – I even started to hate Rebecca . . . I thought she was on your side, against me. When all the time it was just that she trusted you, and I didn't. Please say you'll make it up.'

'Make it up?' Tish was feeling rather dazed by all this, and full of joy. 'Of course I will. Clever old Rebecca. How on earth did she do it?'

'I don't know. Oh, Tish, let's get her and hear all about it and go and buy some stuff and have a party in the dormitory tonight! I feel like blowing my whole allowance in one big bang! I'll tell Jenny and Joanna the whole sordid story, and they'll tell the rest of the team, and they'll all see that you're really a *saint* and –'

'No, don't let's. No parties,' said Tish briefly. She was frowning. 'Nicola Hodges has been a grotty little nuisance, hasn't she?'

'Well, yes –' Sue felt flattened.

'You didn't do much practice this afternoon. Hadn't you better get over to the Hilary and make up for lost time? You've got the rest of the evening.'

'If you think I should – yes.'

Sue was disconcerted. Tish, turning down the chance of a party! Just when they had something marvellous to celebrate. Tish being baffling again! Well, she wasn't going to question it. She was glad to have Tish back on any terms. But it was curious, just the same.

TWELVE
Headline News

For the next few weeks, Rebecca and Sue continued to be baffled by Tish from time to time. It wasn't that things weren't going well. They were going marvellously.

Once she had got the Nicola affair right out of her system, Sue threw herself into her music with complete dedication. All of that very early enthusiasm she'd felt, wanting to be the Music Scholar for this year, returned in abundance. Rebecca explained to the hockey team that Sue had been conned by Nicola Hodges, though she spared them the gory details, and they could see it was true. Tish had known what was best for Sue all along. The glow on Sue's face as she went about her scholarship work proved that. When she wasn't over at the Hilary, dashing away at her fiddle, she was playing back tapes of herself on Tish's cassette recorder, over and over again, anxiously asking the opinion of people like Mara, who had a good ear for music.

All that apart, it was quite obvious that Rebecca and Sue and Tish were just as close as they'd ever been. By the Wednesday morning Sue was sitting next to Rebecca in class again, with Tish just across the gangway, whispering and cracking jokes and passing notes between the three of them, as ever. The Nathan twins were quite pleased to be reunited after two whole days apart.

Neither the team nor Miss Willis were exactly pleased to lose Sue from the Under-14, but they accepted it as inevitable. After the misunderstanding surrounding the first cup match, the team wanted to make it up to Tish. They took to the field for the second cup match, against Caxton High School, in the mood to win. It was a resounding victory, five goals to one in Trebizon's favour. It had been an inspired idea of Tish's to move Laura Wilkins from centre half to left inner, for three of those goals were scored by Laura.

They were back in the Gold Cup with a real

chance and the joyful letter they received from Joss Vining, in hospital, was pinned on the noticeboard to spur them on.

In the third cup match, against a very good team, they drew one all, so everything depended on their fourth and final match in Group Two against Helenbury. Not only must they defeat Helenbury, but they must score at least four goals. If they could do it, that would make them winners of Group Two! They would then go through to play the winners of Group One in the final of the Gold Cup.

The Helenbury match was immediately after half-term, which Rebecca had spent with her grandmother. Sue, along with other scholarship candidates, had remained at Trebizon over the half-term holiday for extra music study. There was only a week to go now until the scholarship. Sue seemed very happy. But Judy Sharp, on the other hand, came back to school in the depths of misery.

Her troublesome ankle, which had held out so well for the packed hockey programme up to half-term, was swollen and painful after a weekend's skiing on some high ground near her home! She was out of the Helenbury match.

Tish immediately switched Rebecca to Judy's

right wing position. Miss Willis, with Tish's agreement, persuaded Mr Barrington to allow Sue to miss orchestra practice – just this once – and she was back in her old position of right inner. It was a home match and not only were Juniper House allowed to turn out to support the team, but some of the older girls were let off lessons as well. Rebecca was keyed up. She had not been playing badly for the team, but she had never really adjusted to an inside-forward position, finding in-field play too crowded for her liking. As a born sprinter she longed for the wide open spaces on the wing. She wanted to shine against Helenbury – and she did!

It was a most thrilling match with the score standing at three all only five minutes before the end. Tish, Sue and Laura had all scored. But they needed four goals – to win the match and to top the table on goals – if they were to qualify for the final! Just when hope was fading, Sue won a tussle for the ball with the opposing centre-half, started to run up-field and then – about to be tackled – shot the ball out to Rebecca. Rebecca was already racing up the field with her opposing wing half in hot pursuit, and caught the ball on her stick in mid-stride, accelerating past a helpless opponent. Her speed was untouchable all the way up the wing and the crack of stick on ball as she whacked it hard into goal, from the very edge of the circle, made the sweetest sound.

They had won! They were through to the final!

But Tish was still baffling.

On that particular evening, for instance, she decided, halfway through the celebration at Moffatt's, to go to bed early! She just seemed suddenly to switch off, exactly as she had the night Rebecca stayed at Sue's house at the end of the Christmas holidays. But at least, on that occasion, she had waited until the party was over.

These odd moods came and went – and were nearly always in the evening. She would be grinning around the place as usual during the day. It seemed to Rebecca that Tish was like someone carrying a burden. It felt light enough in the morning, but sometimes it got heavy by nightfall.

The other strange thing about her was that she started going to the library a lot. Rebecca had always loved the library, in the old manor part of the school, overlooking the parkland. It housed some wonderful books, and she nearly always did her prep there. But not Tish. Her thing was to dash through prep as quickly as possible in the form room, or maybe the Common Room if it were just reading, and then shoot off and do things, like playing badminton over at the sports centre or table tennis down in the Hobbies Room.

Now Tish went to the library nearly every day. Not to read books – but newspapers! Trebizon took daily newspapers, the important-looking, serious ones, and they were laid out on a big table in the library. Tish used to read them all the way through, even the city pages and the sports pages, though she never seemed to know what was in them afterwards! She just said she found she liked them. Rebecca and Sue were utterly baffled.

Everything became crystal clear on the day of the music scholarship. The timing of the whole thing was, in fact, rather extraordinary.

Three adjudicators from London, who had close connections with the school, had travelled down to Trebizon on the Monday night. The scholarship examination would take place on Tuesday morning, over in the Hilary Camberwell Music School. The five candidates would have to play the pieces they'd prepared and do aural and theory tests. They'd also have to play a piece on sight, which meant playing music that they'd never seen before. Sue had spent a lot of time practising her 'sight reading' as that was the thing she found hardest.

After the formal examination the girls would then have lunch with the visitors, over in the Principal's house, and would no doubt be subjected to further scrutiny. Then they would return to school for normal afternoon lessons, while the experts added up the points scored and came to their decision.

As soon as the successful candidate's parents or guardian had been contacted by telephone and informed of the result, she herself would be told – probably during the course of the afternoon.

'Good luck, Sue!' said Tish, after Assembly on Tuesday morning. 'Just think, you're missing maths, biology, French and history! See you after lunch!'

The five candidates were waiting with their instruments in the entrance hall of Juniper House, faces washed and hair brushed. Sue's shoulder-length hair was gleaming and she looked spruce, but Nicola Hodges put them all in the shade. She had taken her flaxen hair out of plaits and it fell to her shoulders in lovely little waves against the dark blue background of her school jumper. She looked suitably nervous, like an anxious little cherub, and at her most appealing. She had been working very hard all term and had kept right out of Sue's way since the day of the big showdown. The other three candidates, with their clarinets and flute, were all tall Second Year girls like Sue, and beside them Nicola looked small and dainty.

'Good luck, Sue,' echoed Rebecca.

Mrs Borrelli arrived with Mr Hobday, the woodwind teacher, and they took their five pupils off to the music school. Everyone but Sue had received flowers and good luck telegrams from their families. It seemed that her parents hadn't thought of it.

'Do you think she minds?' Rebecca asked Tish, as they went off to lessons.

'I'm sure she doesn't!' said Tish. 'She wouldn't be half so relaxed if they'd made a fuss.'

The casual manner that she had adopted in front of Sue had already disappeared and she became quite tense during the morning.

'Relax, yourself!' said Rebecca, after biology. 'Anyone would think *you* were taking the scholarship, not Sue!'

'I feel as though I am,' said Tish.

She didn't eat much at dinner time and straight afterwards said:

'I'm going to the library.'

'Oh no,' thought Rebecca. 'Not the newspapers again.'

But she trailed after Tish and settled down with a book by the big french windows. The library was a lovely, comfortable place. Outside, violent gusts of wind were catching up stray tendrils of ivy and rattling them against the glass. March was coming in like a lion.

Over at the big table, Tish was scanning through a large newspaper. Then suddenly she groaned.

'Ssssh!' said the prefect on duty, and turned back

to rearranging some books on a shelf. But Rebecca looked across towards Tish in alarm. She was staring at something in the newspaper and looking strange.

Rebecca tiptoed over. Tish tried to cover something up with her hands, but Rebecca forced them away. The newspaper was open at the financial pages, and there were two small headlines:

METTERNEX (GLASSWARE) DEALINGS SUSPENDED

HOWARD MURDOCH COMES UNDER FIRE

Rebecca read the news item in a hurry, not understanding some of it. But the main message was clear. Sue's father's company had crashed, its shares had become worthless overnight, and people had lost their savings.

She closed the newspaper and dragged Tish outside.

'You've been waiting for this, Tish! You knew?'

'I didn't know for certain.'

She sank down at the foot of the main staircase in old building, sitting on the bottom stair, and Rebecca sat beside her. Above them the magnificent muralled walls towered up to the ornate moulding of the ceiling above. Tish stared up at the chandeliers, moving almost imperceptibly as a draught whistled through a high-up window. She was very upset.

'My legs feel weak, do yours?'

'A bit. How are Sue's legs going to feel?'

'This means they've lost everything,' said Tish soberly. 'When I was there in the holidays, her parents were sinking every penny they had into the company to try and save it. They'd mortgaged the house, the cars, furniture, paintings, jewellery – the lot. Mr Murdoch thought he could stop the crash.'

'How did you find out?' asked Rebecca. The mystery of Tish's baffling behaviour was solved at last! Everything fell into place.

'It was the most stupid thing,' said Tish. 'It was the night I arrived. The boys were chasing me, we were fooling around, and I went and hid from them – behind the long curtains in the little sitting room. Then suddenly Mr and Mrs Murdoch came in and they shut the door and he said: "Well, darling, the bankers have agreed to an enormous loan, but I've had to put the house and everything else in hock to get it!" I was stuck there, behind the curtains, just frozen to the spot. I didn't dare move or breathe after that. Mrs Murdoch was very nervy and kept asking him what would happen if it didn't work. And he said: "It's got to work. If I can't save Metternex a lot of little people are going to be ruined." He's a good person, really, Rebecca.'

'Did they say anything about Sue?'

'Just touched on it. Mrs Murdoch said, "If it doesn't work, what about the children? The boys will be all right but Sue will have to leave Trebizon." And he replied, "I'm afraid so, but for heaven's sake let's look on the bright side" or something like that. Rebecca, that was the most horrible ten minutes of my life.'

There was silence. Rebecca gazed at Tish. What an amazing person she was. She had been carrying this burden around with her all term, hoping things might come right, dreading that they wouldn't. What a weight – and she'd carried it quite alone!

'You should have told me –' she began.

'I've been longing to! But how could I? It was bad enough me having to put on an act all the time, just imagine both of us at it!'

'You did it pretty well,' said Rebecca, in awe. 'The way you handled the music scholarship – making Sue see it was important, and yet never once letting her suspect . . . I could never have kept it up . . . Oh,

Tish, what you must have been through.'

'The scholarship!' said Tish. 'As far as Sue's concerned, it's her only chance. If she's won it, she won't have to leave Trebizon. Otherwise –' Tish couldn't bring herself to finish the sentence.

'It must be over now,' realised Rebecca. 'Supposing she'd got wind of this before she went in there this morning!'

'She'd have gone to pieces,' said Tish.

Miss Gates, the maths mistress, appeared at the top of the wide staircase and gazed down at them.

'What do you two girls think you're doing –' she asked pleasantly. 'Since when you have been allowed to sit on the main stairs?'

The girls got up and walked away.

'Sue should be back soon. Let's go and wait for her.'

'Are we going to tell her?' asked Rebecca.

'I think we should. Obviously her parents will be writing or telephoning, but when? She could easily hear it from some big-mouth. I think she'd rather hear it from us than from Debbie Rickard or someone.'

Sue arrived back at Juniper House just before two o'clock.

'It was quite good fun!' she told them. 'I quite enjoyed some bits of it – I never thought I would. And you should've seen the lunch they've just given us at Miss Welbeck's house! Talk about two classes of citizen at Trebizon – why can't they make school dinners like that –'

'Sue,' said Rebecca.

They told her everything. It was a tremendous shock and Sue swayed as though she were going to faint. Rebecca and Tish helped her up to the sick room, and Matron made her lie down.

'Just let her be quiet with me for a while,' said Matron.

They returned immediately after games. Sue was sitting up, the colour back in her cheeks. In spite of her obvious distress, she managed to raise a smile. Matron had fetched the offending newspaper and it was lying on the bed. 'No wonder they didn't have time to think about flowers,' Sue said. And then she added: 'I think my father has behaved very correctly and I think I can bear almost anything, as long as I'm able to stay on at Trebizon. If I *have* won, they will know where to find me, won't they?' she asked anxiously.

'We've told Miss Morgan,' said Rebecca.

There was silence and they listened to the ticking of the clock.

By now the judges would certainly have come to their decision. It was simply a matter of the Principal contacting the winning girl's parents, and then informing the girl herself. Why was nothing happening?

At tea time Sue came with the others to the dining hall, though she ate very little. After tea they went back to Juniper House. Still nobody had heard anything.

'It didn't take as long as this last year,' said Mara Leonodis, who had a good memory for anything connected with music. 'Don't you remember Moyra Milton's friends coming into the dining hall at tea time, dancing in a long line, after they'd heard she'd got it!'

Tish and Sue remembered that dance, though not the reason for it. The Third Years, who were Second Years then, had knocked a jug of milk off a table and got into trouble.

'I wonder what the delay is?' Tish said.

'It must be very close,' said Mara. 'It must be neck and neck. Perhaps the judges are having an argument.' She and Rebecca exchanged wary looks as they thought about Nicola Hodges and all her charms.

Sue was very quiet. As yet, none of the others knew just what the scholarship meant to her. No one had any idea that Howard Murdoch was now a bankrupt man. Sue had missed games and gone to lie down in the sick room, and that was all they knew.

The friends sat down on the sofa in the common room, Sue in the middle. They put their arms round her, and waited.

THIRTEEN
The Result of the Music Scholarship

They waited an hour. No news came through. It was awful. Then they learnt that the judges had gone back to London before tea. Someone had seen them go! So it *must* be decided. What had gone wrong?

Sue watched the minute hand of her watch creeping slowly, slowly round. Her head was bent, her hair flopping dejectedly.

'The only thing I can think,' she said, almost inaudibly, 'is that no one's up to standard this year. When that happens, they don't award it . . .'

Her voice trailed away.

'Stuff!' said Tish. But she was scared.

'I think I'll go to bed early,' said Sue. 'I don't

know what's the matter with me. I feel terribly tired, all of a sudden.'

'Doing a Tish on us!' said Rebecca suddenly.

'That's right,' said Sue. 'She's had quite a load to carry this term hasn't she?'

'St Tish!' said the same, with an embarrassed laugh.

'Don't laugh, Tish,' said Sue. She walked towards the door. 'It hasn't really been funny for you, has it?'

'No,' agreed Tish. 'Nor Rebecca.'

'It hasn't been funny for any of us,' said Rebecca. 'Especially that dirty election. Come to think of it, *that* wasn't very saintly.'

'Even saints can be as tough as old boots,' said Sue. 'She just wasn't taking any chances.'

'Let's hope it's all been worth it,' shrugged Tish. She was thinking – 'Surely it can't be because no one's good enough this year? There must be some other reason! Why haven't we heard yet?'

'Yes,' said Rebecca. And she was thinking – 'Why is it taking so long? Is it something to do with Nicola? Please let Sue win.'

And Sue just said:

'I'm going to bed.'

* * *

Mrs Murdoch's car was racing along the motorway in the fast lane, heading west. What time was it lights out at Trebizon these days? It had been eight-thirty in her day. She was going to miss this car. It would have to be handed over to the bank, along with the house and everything else. She must see Sue before she went to bed! It was no use writing or phoning, she must *see* her. She'd telephoned the boys at their school; they were going to be all right. With the money their grandfather had left them, they would just scrape through.

But not Sue. There was no way they could keep her at Trebizon now. She had to break the news to her gently, put her arms round her . . . tell her what had happened to her father . . . tell her, before she found out some other way.

Wasn't it round about now she was hoping to be a Trebizon Music Scholar? What an irony if she were elected, just when she had to leave. It was such a distinction – free music tuition – special opportunities, no doubt. But that wasn't going to pay the fees. *Come on, come on. Must get there.*

At least Howard was resting. After working through the night and most of the morning, he'd let her drive him down to friends in the country, where he could get some much needed sleep and escape the phone for a few hours. He was a very exhausted man.

At a quarter to nine, when the car screeched to a halt in front of the main Trebizon building, Mrs Murdoch was on the edge of exhaustion herself. She got out and stared up through the shadows at the façade of the lovely manor house. The wind lifted up the edges of her headscarf. There was a light still burning in the Principal's study, upstairs, and a soft glow coming from the tall windows of the library on the ground floor. She could see some senior girls moving around inside. Two had their heads together, bent over a book. She felt a wave of nostalgia for her own schooldays at Trebizon and then, thinking of Sue, a great sadness.

'Mrs Murdoch?'

Entering the building, she was amazed to see the Principal of Trebizon School descending the main staircase, a hand stretched out in greeting. Mrs Murdoch had meant to telephone the school to warn them that she was coming, and for a moment she wondered if she'd done so after all! Everything today had been such a frantic rush . . .

'I've just been trying to telephone you,' said Miss Welbeck.

'To telephone *me*?'

They met at the foot of the stairs.

'You've driven down to see Susan?'

'Yes! I'm sorry, I should have let you know. Will she have gone to bed? I wanted to break some news to her . . .' Mrs Murdoch lowered her eyes. 'I didn't want her to hear it by chance.'

'About Metternex? She does know about that,' said Miss Welbeck. 'We've been trying to contact you about something else. Since three o'clock this afternoon, as a matter of fact, at both the telephone numbers that you gave on the form –'

'The form, Miss Welbeck?'

'The entry form for the Hilary Camberwell Music Scholarship. I need hardly tell you that the five candidates are in great suspense, waiting to hear the result of the competition, and none of them more so than your daughter. But, of course, we never inform the winner until her parents have been told and the scholarship has been formally accepted on her behalf.'

'Then –?' Mrs Murdoch felt only dismay.

'Susan was a clear twenty points ahead of her nearest rival in the competition this morning. Are you willing that she be elected the Hilary Camberwell

Music Scholar for this year?'

Mrs Murdoch shook her head. She felt like weeping. She had driven all the way from London – to hear this!

'I'm sorry, Miss Welbeck –'

'You do realise, of course, that the scholarship carries with it free music tuition and up to full fees for the rest of a girl's time at the school?'

'Full fees?' gasped Mrs Murdoch. 'No. No, I – I hadn't realised.'

'I thought perhaps you hadn't,' said Miss Welbeck. At last her face had relaxed into a smile. 'I suggest we go across to Juniper House and break the good news to your daughter. We may, of course, have to ask Matron to wake her up first.'

But Sue was not asleep when Matron walked in and told her to put her dressing gown on and come downstairs. Neither were Rebecca, nor Tish, nor any of the occupants of dormitory number six. All the girls now knew about Sue's father. It just had to come out. And they had been discussing, endlessly, the question of the scholarship.

'Your mother's driven all the way down from London to see you. Miss Welbeck has brought her over and they're waiting to see you downstairs,' said

Matron. She couldn't hide her excitement. 'I think they've both got a very nice piece of news for you, after all that bad news you've had today.'

One look at Matron's smiling face was enough.

As Sue scrambled into her dressing gown and stumbled towards the door, Tish ran after her. She was laughing and crying at the same time.

'Your glasses, Sue!' And then: 'You've done it, Sue! You've won!'

When Sue had gone, Tish turned on her cassette recorder and it played some music at full volume. She grabbed hold of Rebecca's hand and together they raced round and round the dormitory, jumping over beds, whooping with joy. To complete their happiness, they then had their first good pillow fight for weeks, and the rest of dormitory number six joined in.

FOURTEEN
How the Wishes Turned Out

Rebecca didn't get her wish. She didn't stay in the Under-14 hockey team. Her second term at Trebizon had its disappointments, as well as its surprises.

For the final of the Gold Cup, against Skinnerton School, Dorset, Rebecca was dropped from the Trebizon team and wasn't even a reserve. Judy's ankle was completely better and she was back as right wing. Sue was back as right inner. Right-half Eleanor Keating, one of the four First Years now in the team, showed unexpected brilliance as a winger in one of the practice games. If anything went wrong with Judy, Tish realised, she could substitute Eleanor. So – after much heart-searching – she picked another defence player to join Verity Williams as a reserve. 'The slightest chink in our defence, and we've had it,' she explained to Rebecca. 'I've got to have strong replacements lined up for Robert or Joanna or Sheila – or the Skinnies will be in there scoring! Their centre forward's quite a girl!'

The final was played at a neutral ground, outside Exeter, and three coachloads from Trebizon went to cheer. Trebizon's tactics were defensive ones – the opposing centre-forward couldn't get near the ball. Then Tish broke through after half-time and scored the only goal of the match.

Trebizon had won the West of England Junior Gold Cup, against older teams, for the first time ever! Rebecca cheered until she was hoarse. At the end Tish, having been presented with the cup, walked over and gave it to somebody who was sitting in a chair near the touchline, wrapped up warmly. Joss Vining had just come out of hospital, and her parents had driven her to Exeter to see the final.

Singing loudly in the coach on the way back, Rebecca remembered that inspired goal she had managed to score against Helenbury, which had got them to the final. That had been *her* moment of glory and she would always cherish it!

The main surprises of the term had been those

created by Tish's baffling behaviour – that went without saying. But another surprise for Rebecca, the one when Juniper House had decided to submit her essay to the school magazine, turned out to be even more thrilling than she had contemplated. When the spring term edition of *The Trebizon Journal* was delivered from the printers, in a lovely glossy blue and white cover, Rebecca found that 'A Winter's Morning' had been set up right across the centre pages, and was delicately illustrated with line drawings. They had been done by Pippa Fellowes-Walker, and were so good they made Rebecca admire her all the more.

Audrey Maxwell and her editorial committee then decided to submit Rebecca's essay to a national newspaper competition for the best work published in a school magazine. It won Third Prize and at prize-giving, towards the end of term, Rebecca had to go up to receive a framed certificate from Miss Welbeck, in front of the whole school.

'The first day you arrived at Trebizon, do you remember Rebecca, I told you to aim high?' smiled the Principal, firmly clasping her by the hand. 'Well done. Keep it up.'

Rebecca shook a strand of hair out of her eyes.

Could that really have been her, that funny new girl of last September, so anxious to make her mark at Trebizon?

Prizes were given in alphabetical order and straight after Rebecca came Sue, to be presented with her Hilary Camberwell badge. As Miss Welbeck fastened on the distinctive piece of jewellery, there was some very special applause for Sue.

Another person to receive a surprise that term was Nicola Hodges. She came up to Rebecca, a week after the result of the music scholarship had been announced, and spoke to her in honeyed tones.

'Have you still got that cassette?' she asked.

'Tish has got it,' said Rebecca.

'Well, I was wondering –' Nicola smiled her most appealing smile, '– now that it's all over, could you rub it clean please?'

'Has your mother stopped boasting?' inquired Rebecca.

'She's talking about next year now,' said Nicola.

'Well, remember what I told you,' said Rebecca. 'Tell her to shut up.'

'But what about that tape?' asked Nicola anxiously. 'Those things I said to Sue. Can you rub them off now?'

'There's nothing to rub off,' said Rebecca. 'The tape was blank.'

She walked away, leaving Nicola rooted to the spot.

On the last morning of term, the three friends packed their trunks after breakfast and then went down the path through the trees, for a last look at the bay.

They watched the waves breaking against the sea shore.

'None of our wishes came true!' Tish said suddenly. 'Sue wanted to be head of games, and she's ended up Music Scholar. Rebecca wanted to be in the team and she's ended up winning a prize for writing, instead . . .'

'That's the way it goes,' said Rebecca. 'And what was *your* secret wish? Though I think I can guess.'

'I just wanted Sue's father to save Metternex,' said Tish.

'You can't say he didn't try,' observed Sue. She would be going home to a much smaller, rented house. 'You can't change fate, though. *Que sera, sera . . .* whatever will be, will be. It just goes to show that all three of us wished for the very things that were impossible.'

'Doesn't everyone?' said Tish. 'There's something upside-down about life. Nothing ever turns out quite how you expect.'

'Yes,' agreed Rebecca. She thought of that party at Sue's lovely big house in the Christmas holidays. Who would ever have dreamt that it was Nicola's father who was rolling in money and Sue's father who was going broke! But that was all history now. And, one day, Sue's father would be successful again. Rebecca felt sure of that.

'Come on, you two,' she said. 'You've got to get your train and I've got to get my bus.'

Her parents weren't able to come home for Easter. She was going to her grandmother's once more. As she ran to the top of a sand dune and waited, she could smell that spring was in the air. In the little wood behind her the birds were twittering; soon the trees would be bursting into leaf again. In front of her the sea looked quite blue for once, the sun dazzling on to it. March had come in like a lion, but now it was going out like a lamb.

Rebecca had joined the school Gardening Club and sown things in the big walled garden behind the stable block: lettuce, parsley, onions, leeks, carrots and spinach. She hoped they would grow well! Mrs Dalzeil, who was in charge of home economics, had promised to teach them how to make delicious soups from vegetables they had grown themselves, next term! She was also going to show them how to prepare things for the freezer.

The other two joined her up on top of the dune.

'You'll like the summer term, Becky,' said Tish. 'The sea's warm enough to swim in . . . and there's tennis . . . and picnics and . . .'

'Exams!' laughed Sue.

'. . . and athletics,' finished Tish.

'I like the sound of athletics!' said Rebecca.

The long bus journey to Gloucestershire was a peaceful interlude. Rebecca thought about home and she thought about the past term and she tried to imagine the summer term. She would enjoy the Easter holidays while they lasted and soon she would be seeing all her friends again. Tish, and Sue, and Mara and Elf and Margot. And Joss would be back. And of course – there was Pippa. She liked her more than ever now.

It would be her third term.

Summer Term at TREBIZON

Read about
Rebecca's
third term
at **TREBIZON**
in this special
extract...

<u>ONE</u>
A Maths Problem

For Rebecca Mason there were going to be a lot of good things about the summer term at Trebizon – and a few bad ones, too. The bad things all seemed to have a connection with the letter 'M'.

M stood for maths. It also stood for Maxwell. Worst of all, it stood for Mason, her own surname, and that was going to create its own problems.

Rebecca suspected none of this as the long distance bus trundled through the green English countryside. She had spent the Easter holidays at her grandmother's home in Gloucestershire, one of a group of 'retirement bungalows' on a small housing estate. She loved her gran but she had missed seeing London and her parents. The London house was let out until July, and her parents were in Saudi

Arabia. Her father had been posted there by his firm the previous September and Rebecca had been transferred from her local day school to Trebizon, a boarding school in the west country. She had been lonely there at first, until she had made some friends. Her two best friends were Tish Anderson and Sue Murdoch.

Now she was travelling back to Trebizon for the summer term, and although to her grandmother she had pretended to groan about going back to school, she was secretly quite looking forward to it.

As yet, the letter 'M' had no significance in her life. She couldn't have cared less what letter her surname began with. As for Mr Maxwell-beginning-with-M (who liked to be called Max), she had never even met him. So that left only maths.

She did spare a few brief thoughts to those, as well she might in view of the warning letter she had had from her father. The question of maths crossed her mind as, her luggage having been transferred from the coach at Trebizon Bus Station to a waiting taxi, she was being driven at speed out of the top end of town in the direction of school. Rebecca's thoughts lingered just long enough on the subject of maths to wish that they had never been invented, then quickly passed on.

There was Trebizon Bay! As the taxi passed the last of the hotels on the fringe of the town and turned into open country she could see the waters of the big, blue bay in the distance, across the fields. Although it was still only the end of April, there was a glorious sun this afternoon, dazzling on the sea, and the air was warm. Rebecca knew that they were allowed to swim in the sea during the summer term.

'I wonder if we'd be allowed to today, after tea?' she thought. She felt sticky after her long journey. 'I'd like that.' She wound down the window of the taxi half-way and stuck her head out, so that the rushing air blew her long fair hair around her face. Now she could just glimpse the school buildings in the parkland over on the west side of the bay, old roofs and white stone gables amongst tall trees that had recently burst into leaf. Trebizon School was still there then, as solid as ever.

Soon the taxi turned in through the main school gates, slowed down to ten m.p.h., as instructed, then dawdled along the long leafy lane that led to the main school building, which had once been a manor house. They passed one or two cars coming from the direction of the school, but most girls had arrived back in the early afternoon. The taxi-driver knew the ropes and crawled straight past old school and right round behind the dining hall block, eventually pulling up in the cobbled yard at the back of Juniper House: the long red-brick boarding house where all the junior girls at Trebizon, including Rebecca, lived. The driver opened the rear door of the taxi while Rebecca got out, arms laden with carrier bags and a tennis racket, the overspill from her trunk.

'Rebecca!' shrieked several voices at once.

'Tish!' laughed Rebecca. 'Sue! Mara –!'

They were all running towards her. In front was Ishbel Anderson, Tish for short, her dark curly hair badly in need of a comb. Behind her Sue Murdoch, Mara Leonodis and Margot Lawrence looked equally dishevelled. They had just finished a game of tennis and were carrying rackets. 'Elf' – chubby Sally Elphinstone – brought up the rear, carrying some tennis balls. She had been keeping score and was not sweaty and untidy like the others.

'About time you got here,' said Tish.

'It was that bus again,' said Rebecca. 'What a journey!'

'Where's this to, miss?' asked the taxi-driver. He was getting Rebecca's trunk out of the large boot.

'Upstairs?'

'Second floor!' interjected Sue promptly. 'Dormitory number six. We'll show you. You won't believe this but she's supposed to be unpacked by tea time!'

Sue led the way to the back door of Juniper House, followed by three of them, chattering. Tish hung back with Rebecca and the taxi man and yelled out:

'Catch, Margot!'

She hurled her tennis racket through the air as the black girl turned swiftly. Deftly Margot caught it.

'Now I can help you hump this trunk upstairs,' said Tish to the man.

With a great deal of awkwardness and laughter she did so, once colliding with Rebecca who was just behind them so that Rebecca dropped her things all over the stairs. Tish seemed to think that was hilarious. On the second floor landing they picked their way through the empty cases and trunks that were waiting to be collected and at last deposited the trunk safely inside dormitory six, at the foot of Rebecca's bed.

'Thanks!' said the taxi-driver to Tish. 'Your friend

can get unpacked now.'

Rebecca dumped her other things on her bed and scrabbled around to find her purse. She paid the taxi-driver self-consciously, as she was not very used to hiring taxis, and just guessed wildly when it came to the tip, hoping it was neither too generous nor too mean.

'Thank you, miss,' he said, to Rebecca's relief. He thought she seemed a pretty youngster, athletic-looking, too. He glanced at the tennis racket on her bed and winked. 'You off to Wimbledon then?'

'Some hopes!' laughed Rebecca, blushing.

'Rebecca's going to be a sprinter!' said Tish.

'A sprinter, eh? You'll have your eye on the Olympics then.'

They all laughed, and as he left Elf called out:

'Someone in our form really has been to Wimbledon. Junior Wimbledon.'

'Hope she got a good seat,' he observed.

'No –' Elf started to follow him. 'She *played* there –'

'Now, now, Elf,' said Sue, hauling her back. 'He knows. Stop showing off about Joss. She wouldn't like it.'

'How is Joss?' asked Rebecca. 'Seen her yet?'

Josselyn Vining was head of games in the junior house, but had been away most of last term after a minor back operation.

'Fitter than ever!' said Sue. 'Saw her down on the courts –'

'Beating Miss Willis,' added Tish.

Rebecca sighed. It must be very satisfying to be like Joss Vining, brilliant at any game she turned her hand to and a natural leader. Or was it? It must set you just a little apart from everyone else.

All five girls rallied round to help Rebecca get unpacked at speed, then dragged her empty trunk out on to the landing just as the first tea bell went. There were squeals then and a stampede into the washroom; hands and faces were washed and hair combed, Rebecca's included.

'Nice to see you back, Rebecca,' said Mara, waiting for her comb.

'Nice to *be* back,' confessed Rebecca.

Even better than being like Josselyn Vining, Rebecca decided, was being one of a crowd. Tish and Sue were her best friends because dramatic happenings in her first two terms had drawn them very close together. But the other three, Mara Leonodis, Margot Lawrence and Sally Elphinstone, were the sort Rebecca liked too. They all joined forces sometimes, especially when things needed doing – the 'Action Committee' Tish called it – and they certainly got things done. There were two other girls in the dormitory, both very pleasant, but it was these five she was with now that Rebecca liked best of all.

'I wonder if we'll need the Action Committee for anything this term?' said Rebecca, working furiously at a tangle.

'Only Charity Week,' said Mara.

'Charity Week?'

'Yes,' smiled Mara. 'And that'll be enough excitement for me.' There was a light in the Greek girl's eyes. 'This term I'm going to work very, very hard.'

'You *are*?' exclaimed Tish, with interest.

Mara had to burst out with it.

'If I work very hard, I may go into the A stream when we move up into the Third Year next term! It was in my report!'

'Oh, Mara!'

'Great!'

They all crowded round, patting Mara on the back. They were all Second Years at present and in the same form together, II Alpha, with the sole exception of Mara, who was in II Beta. She so much wanted to be in the same form as the rest of them. Now perhaps, when they moved up into III Alpha, Mara would be joining them!

'Anything wrong, Rebeck?' asked Tish, a moment later.

There was a funny look on Rebecca's face, for she had been reminded of something that she distinctly wanted to forget. But she quickly shook her head.

'Hey, listen!' said Sue, opening wide the washroom door. 'It's the second bell. We're late!'

They all rushed down the west staircase, out of the front of Juniper House, which overlooked the quadrangle gardens and old school opposite, and along the terrace to the modern dining hall block. The doors were open and the clamour of noise hit Rebecca like a tidal wave. It sounded like four hundred girls talking at once which was, very roughly, the position.

The next day, Wednesday, when the term really started, they would have to sit at their proper tables. Today, girls could sit where they liked. The six latecomers had to take seats where they could find them and Rebecca found herself sitting with Mara and Sue at the same table as Roberta Jones, who had written a play in the Easter holidays.

'I shall be inviting people to be in it,' she said stolidly.

'But what's it for exactly, Roberta?' asked Rebecca.

'For Juniper's Charity Week of course,' said Roberta.

This being Rebecca's first summer at Trebizon, Sue had to explain to her that early in May each year Juniper House organised a Charity Week. All the members of the junior boarding house, the entire First and Second Years, split up into small groups. Each group had to think of a fund raising idea and organize it, outside of lesson times, and then carry it out during the course of the week. 'It's quite fun,' Sue explained. 'There are different things going on every day.'

The girls in the group that raised the most money would get special merit marks from the Principal.

'I see what you mean about the Action Committee now!' said Rebecca, turning to Mara.

'That's a thought,' said Sue. 'We'd be good together. We'll get Tish to revive it, shall we?'

'Let's have a meeting and try and think of something really different,' said Rebecca, pushing her bowl forward for another helping of fruit salad and whipped cream. 'When?'

'I've got to go and do some music practice in a minute,' said Sue.

'I've got to check all my maths holiday work with my new calculator,' said the new, industrious Mara. 'Let's all be thinking of some ideas and talk about it tonight!'

'Right,' agreed Rebecca, but she felt suddenly depressed.

Maths!

Her father's letter came back to her mind with a jolt.

Your maths are letting you down, Becky. You must try very hard next term.

Enclosed with the letter had been a photocopy of her school report, which had been sent out to her parents. On the whole it had been good, but beside *Mathematics* Miss Gates had written: *Generally poor. Some improvement this term but Rebecca has a great deal of ground to make up.*

However, it wasn't that which had filled her with alarm. It was the Principal's comment, right at the bottom of the report:

Rebecca has high ability in some subjects, but unless she makes noticeable progress in maths next term it may be advisable for her to spend the next academic year in the Beta stream, where she can receive extra maths teaching.

(Signed) Madeleine Welbeck. *Principal.*

So, just as Mara was excited at the possibility of going up next year, Rebecca was dismayed at the possibility of going down. No wonder Tish had noticed a funny look on her face. Now Sue noticed something, too.

'Anything wrong?'

'Tell you later.'

Rebecca decided she would tell both Sue and Tish about it, straight after tea. That's what best friends were for. They would find some way of cheering her up.

She was right about that.